GOING ONCE, GOING TWICE

BOOKS BY JAN THOMPSON

Seaside Chapel (7 Books)
JanThompson.com/seaside

Savannah Sweethearts (12 Books)
JanThompson.com/savannah

Vacation Sweethearts (8 Books)
JanThompson.com/vacation

Christmas Sweethearts (3 Books)
JanThompson.com/christmastown

Midtown Christmas (4 Books)
JanThompson.com/christmas

Protector Sweethearts (6 Books)
JanThompson.com/protector

Defender Sweethearts (6 Books)
JanThompson.com/defender

Guardian Sweethearts (4 Books)
JanThompson.com/guardian

Binary Hackers (4 Books)
JanThompson.com/binary

GOING ONCE, GOING TWICE

GUARDIAN SWEETHEARTS
BOOK 3

JAN THOMPSON

GEORGIA
PRESS

GOING ONCE, GOING TWICE (GUARDIAN SWEETHEARTS BOOK 3)

eBook ISBN: 978-1-944188-96-2
Paperback ISBN: 978-1-944188-97-9

To my Lord and Savior, Jesus Christ, who died on the cross to save me from my sins and rose again from the grave to give me eternal life in heaven.

For God so loved the world that He gave His only begotten Son, that whoever believes in Him should not perish but have everlasting life.
—John 3:16

ABOUT GOING ONCE, GOING TWICE

GUARDIAN SWEETHEARTS BOOK 3

An abducted child.
A desperate mother.
A secretive father.

When her four-year-old son is kidnapped, a stay-at-home mother reactivates her hidden skills to mount a rescue operation. Will the kidnapping drive her to the edge?

Phoebe's Fears

Office manager Phoebe O'Tierney's decision to help a single mother earn some childcare income ends up putting her son in grave danger when he is abducted in broad daylight.

The search and rescue would've been like looking for a needle in a haystack, but the human traffickers don't realize that Phoebe has a powerful magnet in the form of connections in high places at Mendenhall Retreat where she works.

Keenan's Call

There's much former Special Forces soldier Keenan O'Tierney wants to tell his wife but can't due to Mendenhall Security company policy. He believes that someone in his working past is exacting revenge on his family.

He needn't have worried about keeping secrets because Phoebe has come to the same conclusion. When Keenan realizes that, he joins her in her mission to rescue their son.

Tropes/Themes:

- Child Abduction
- Vendetta
- Human Trafficking
- Married Life
- Husband and Wife Relationship
- Mountain Retreat
- Great Smoky Mountains
- Metro Atlanta, Georgia

Author's Note: *Going Once, Going Twice* happened six years after *Reach for Me* (Vacation Sweethearts Book 2) ended. In that Christian romance novel with a side of suspense, Phoebe met Keenan at the mountaintop Mendenhall Retreat while they were both in the valleys of their lives. Read *Reach for Me* to find out how they met and fell in love.

Reach for Me (Vacation Sweethearts Book 2)
JanThompson.com/reach

Publisher's Note: An abridged novella edition of *Going Once, Going Twice* debuted in the 12-author *Don't Blink* anthology that was published on October 7, 2025. That boxed set has been unpublished.

GOING ONCE, GOING TWICE

CHAPTER 1

"Are you going to pick up Jamie or do you want me to?" Keenan O'Tierney stood beside Phoebe's desk and sipped more coffee.

When he made a face, Phoebe knew that he'd put too much cream in it—again.

She chuckled. She was still the only person who could make his coffee perfectly for him. Married for six years, she knew a thing or two about her husband's preferences, but he was still a man of secrets when it came to their work at Mendenhall Security.

Well, to be fair, Phoebe's job as the office manager at Mendenhall Retreat precluded her from the daily operations of Mendenhall Security, even though the company headquarters was housed at the retreat center—and also Atlanta, where Keenan would be flying to that evening.

"Aren't you supposed to go home and pack for your weeklong job at the Atlanta branch?" Phoebe sat back in her swivel chair and gazed at her husband.

She was going to miss him for all six of those days, but he'd promised to come home by Saturday night so that he could take her and Jamie to church on Sunday morning. Their four-year-old boy would be singing in the summer kid's camp choir, which would help the choir in the congregational singing in the Sunday morning service.

Keenan put his coffee mug down on Phoebe's table, walked over to her, and pulled her to her feet.

"I don't fly out until midnight."

Keenan wrapped his good arm around Phoebe's waist and buried his face in her neck. "I don't want to go. I'm going to miss you."

Phoebe pushed him back. "We're at work!"

"It's four o'clock. I've been here since six in the morning, and you've been here since seven. We've each worked more than eight hours today." Gently, he let her go.

He had been extra careful to avoid holding Phoebe with his new prosthetic arm because it would be too strong for her. The experimental VenomLabs prosthetic arm was robotic and could crush her spine if something went haywire.

"Pickup is at five, but if you want, we could both go early." Phoebe relented. "That way, you can give him a hug before you go out of town."

Keenan had shared his schedule with her—except for blackout tasks above her clearance—so Phoebe knew that the Mendenhall chopper would pick him up at six o'clock from the helipad behind the Mendenhall Lodge, where the offices were housed.

"My thought exactly." Keenan planted a kiss on Phoebe's forehead.

Phoebe hadn't been a touchy-feely kind of person until she had met Keenan some seven years ago now.

At that time, they had both been hiding in their own valleys of problems, but God brought them together to the mountaintop of peace. One year later, they'd married, and two years afterwards, little Jamie was born.

"It takes twenty minutes to get to Maysie's house from here." Phoebe peeled away. "I'm going to the restroom, and we can leave at 4:30 p.m."

"Because you took thirty minutes—and not a minute more—for lunch today."

"I ate at my desk and worked through lunch."

"So technically you can take precisely thirty minutes off tomorrow's work because you've over-worked by that much time."

Phoebe rolled her eyes. She knew that her husband was only teasing her with his attempt at accuracy. Yes, it was true that she clocked in and clocked out at exact times, but that was only because she didn't want to be late in picking Jamie up from Mrs. Madison's house.

Summer was different in the O'Tierney house-hold. Instead of going to regular K4 like he did during the school year, Jamie spent five hours a day at the summer kid's camp at their church, Misty Mountain Chapel. Maysie would pick him up from day camp and take him home, along with her own son, Hanley, who was only six months older than Jamie.

If Phoebe hadn't trusted Mrs. Madison and her family, she wouldn't have left Jamie in her grand-niece's care.

Phoebe had a long history with the nonagenarian Winnie Madison, known all over town as Mrs. Madison. Before Phoebe had met Keenan, she worked part time at the funeral parlor that Mrs. Madison owned. At that time, Mrs. Madison lived with her other grand-niece, April. After April married and moved out to live near the college where her husband taught, her divorced older sister, Maysie, moved in to take care of Mrs. Madison as her full-time caregiver.

Since Maysie also had a son in the same K4 as Jamie, Phoebe talked to Keenan about paying Maysie to care for Jamie until five o'clock every workday.

Nonetheless, it was only a temporary situation. When summer was over, Mendenhall Retreat would open its own on-site daycare and after-school care for children of staff and guests. Phoebe preferred that arrangement because she could see her son multiple times during the day and free herself from worrying about him.

She felt guilty sometimes that she showered so much love on Jamie. She wished she could do the same for her other biological child that she'd given birth to under traumatic circumstances out of wedlock when she was still young some fourteen years ago. Instead of aborting her, she'd given her up for adoption.

A sweet childless couple raised her daughter in Pigeon Forge, about fifteen minutes from nearby Gatlinburg. They had named her Alexandra, but called her Alexi. They allowed Phoebe to visit her as often as she wanted. Phoebe always brought Jamie with her so that he could spend time with his older sister.

Alexi's adopted father was an associate pastor at a small church in Pigeon Forge, and his wife was a homeschooling mom. They had no other children, but they didn't spoil Alexi as Phoebe had spoiled Jamie. Phoebe had a lot to learn from that godly couple whom God had brought along to raise the child she couldn't.

Before Phoebe knew it, she was standing in front of the mirror in the women's restroom, mindlessly running warm water over her hands. She couldn't remember whether she'd put soap on her hands or not.

I need a break.

Summer might feel like a vacation season to people everywhere, but not to Mendenhall Retreat. It was always busy and always booked. Its guests were not ordinary guests either, but it wasn't Phoebe's place to ask questions.

Sometimes these guests became friends of Mendenhall Retreat, and sometimes they were hired as staff. For example, Joseph Brannigan, the eighty-eight-year-old former special forces soldier, was the current deputy director of the retreat, filling in for Esperanza Diaz-Mendenhall, the owner and director of Mendenhall Retreat, whenever she was out of town.

Not only was Esperanza gone a lot, but Phoebe's own husband was also often away on assignment. Every time he was gone for a week or more, Phoebe would fill her schedule up until the day before he'd be home to keep her busy and take her mind off Keenan.

Their marriage had been a blissful one with few quarrels—which surprised her.

Often, Keenan would yield to her, but there were things that he couldn't talk to her about. Phoebe understood the nature of his work at Mendenhall

Security, but she also wondered—sometimes—if they would be closer to each other if they could speak freely.

Phoebe had talked to her boss about it because Esperanza had been married to a CIA agent, Lamar, before he was brutally murdered in this very retreat center seven years ago. Since Esperanza was a widow now, she couldn't help Phoebe, but she introduced her to Marie Bouchard, who now worked at the Atlanta office of Mendenhall Security.

Marie had once been an INTERPOL agent, and keeping secrets had destroyed her marriage. After they reconciled and remarried, her husband had invested in Mendenhall Security and had enough clearance to be able to ask questions and get answers.

Hmmm...

Maybe that was what Phoebe needed to do. If she could get the same clearance as Keenan at Mendenhall Security, then he wouldn't have to filter or censor any information from her, right?

Esperanza had eyed Phoebe for the deputy director position that Brannigan would vacate soon because he wanted to retire and enjoy life with his wife of seventy years.

Phoebe had been thinking about taking the position, but she didn't want to hasten Brannigan's retirement too soon. She felt that she still had a lot to learn from the octogenarian.

Besides, it would be a leap from office manager to deputy director, even though she had been filling in for Esperanza for years whenever she went out of town. She also knew everything that Brannigan did.

However, now that things had gone too smoothly

between her and Keenan, she felt that it was time for her to learn more about his work so that she could provide support for him when difficult times arose. To do that without clearance would be impossible.

The deputy director position seemed to appeal more and more.

As she dried her hands on paper towels, she felt bad that she had to find a roundabout way to learn more about her husband's work. She wondered if it would've been the same had he been a CIA agent.

She chuckled as she walked out of the women's restroom, straight into Keenan's arms.

He didn't ask her, "What took you so long?"

He simply smiled that affable smile that had attracted her to him in the first place.

"Ready to go?" Keenan asked.

Phoebe nodded.

They held hands and walked down the hallway without a word toward the staff parking lot. Phoebe thought that they both wanted to say something but didn't.

Keenan's phone rang twice, and he took the calls, but didn't say much. He basically okayed his way through the conversation.

Phoebe wanted him to say more so that she could fill in the blanks with her imagination. In her mind, Keenan was a swashbuckling hero who spent his time saving the world without anyone knowing it.

She checked herself. It was not a good idea to put him on so high a pedestal lest he fell from grace one day and disappointed or failed her. God should be on the throne, and not man. She couldn't remember the entire passage, so she looked it up on the Bible app on her phone as they walked to the parking lot.

The afternoon sun shone down on them as Keenan unlocked their pickup truck doors. The gentleman that he was, he opened the passenger side door for Phoebe to climb in without looking up because she was still searching for the verse on her app.

"Thanks," she said. "What's that verse in the Bible that talks about how people disappoint you but God doesn't?"

"Hmm... I think it's in a couple of places." Keenan didn't close the door. "My favorite one is Psalm 20:7."

Keenan recited it.

> Some trust in chariots, and some in horses;
> But we will remember the name of the Lord our God.

"That's a good one." Phoebe put her seatbelt on as Keenan lifted her skirt away from the door before closing it.

However, it wasn't what she was looking for. After Keenan got into the driver's seat and buckled in, Phoebe found it.

"Psalm 146:3-7." Phoebe scrolled on her phone.

"Oh? Read it to me." Keenan backed the pickup truck out of the parking spot and drove out of the parking lot as Phoebe read the passage aloud to him.

> Do not put your trust in princes,
> Nor in a son of man, in whom there is no help.
> His spirit departs, he returns to his earth;

In that very day his plans perish.
Happy is he who has the God of Jacob for his
help,
   Whose hope is in the Lord his God,
   Who made heaven and earth,
   The sea, and all that is in them;
   Who keeps truth forever,
   Who executes justice for the oppressed,
   Who gives food to the hungry.
   The Lord gives freedom to the prisoners.

"Why do I think that God is preparing us for something?" Keenan asked without explaining further.

That was just like him. He couldn't talk about what he would be doing in Atlanta all week, and so whatever it was that God was preparing him for would be something that Phoebe wouldn't find out.

Then again... Phoebe had meant to find a verse to encourage herself to turn her eyes toward Jesus rather than toward Keenan and secrets at work. She ended up sharing a Bible passage that might help Keenan in his upcoming project.

She felt a lift in her heart. "God is always teaching us something."

"I meant that..." Keenan cleared his throat. "Well, you know I can't say much. I can say this, though. Every time I take up an assignment, I worry about not being able to come home to you and Jamie."

Phoebe thought it was interesting that Keenan had also felt the unspoken tension between them too. On the outset, they were a happy couple, but underlying all that facade, they couldn't be entirely transparent with each other behind their own closed doors.

"It's the nature of your work." Phoebe tried to comfort him—and herself.

"Someday I want to retire from Mendenhall Security and stay home. Then we could discuss anything, and I don't have to check myself before I open my mouth."

"You mean that you want to be a stay-at-home dad?"

"Well, I meant that I'd work at the retreat instead of flying all over the world."

"I see. You know that the deputy director's job at the retreat is vacant." Phoebe wanted that job too, but she didn't want to compete with her husband for the same position. She'd keep her office manager job if Keenan wanted the deputy director role.

Phoebe determined in her heart to yield. It would bring Keenan home, where it was safe.

Then again, Keenan might get bored running the retreat and watching other special operators and former military people come here to rest and recover from their injuries and then go back to the field for more rounds.

Before Phoebe realized it, they had driven past the Breckenridge B&B. This meant that they were just a few traffic lights away from Mrs. Madison's house.

"Truth be told, the deputy director is doing too much. You see what Joe does every day, right? His official position is deputy director—because Espy is the director—but he's also the chief of security for the retreat."

"When Mendenhall Retreat was small, some seven or eight years ago, Espy was here all the time, so the deputy director hardly had anything to do. Joe spent all his time in the security room," Phoebe recalled. "However, since Espy opened a new branch in Atlanta, she's been away a lot. Joe's deputy director job is no longer part time because he wears two hats."

"I forgot to tell you that I talked to Espy about splitting the job into two," Keenan said. "I suggested that she hire someone else to be the chief of security."

"Let me guess. So she offered you the job."

Keenan chuckled. "Next time I'll remember to be careful what I suggest."

"You'd be perfect for the role. Then you can stay home and drive a golf cart to work."

"We can wake up together every morning instead of in different cities, states, or countries." Keenan sighed. "I'm tired of traveling."

"I'm tired for you."

With the position of deputy director, Phoebe could get top clearance so that Keenan could speak to her freely about his work without censoring himself.

Ironically, if Keenan took up the chief of security position at the retreat, he wouldn't be traveling away on missions anymore, so what was there to hide?

"Let's pray for God's perfect will to prevail," Phoebe said.

"Good prayer." Keenan parked in the Madison driveway. "How about we pray now?"

And so they did. After the brief prayer for God's guidance for their careers, Phoebe got out of the passenger side before Keenan could come around to get her. They walked together to the front porch and rang the doorbell.

Nobody answered.

Phoebe rang it again and knocked on the door as loudly as she could with the brass knocker.

Still, nobody answered.

"Uh-oh." Phoebe turned to Keenan.

He was the epitome of calm. No expression registered on his face. Not even a furrowed brow or a worried look. His face was as cool as a marble head.

However, as soon as he looked down at the brown welcome mat, his eyes widened at the streaks of dark liquid.

"Someone spilled something?" Phoebe smelled blood as soon as she said it.

A Glock had appeared in Keenan's left hand, his only biological limb. The other hand was empty, and that made Phoebe slightly relieved. She didn't want to see an armed robotic prosthetic hand at all.

He ushered her off the porch, stepping onto the flower bed behind an exterior wall.

"I'll text Maysie." She did, but Maysie didn't reply. She texted one more time. Still nothing.

"Get back in the truck, drive away, and call 911," Keenan whispered.

For the first time ever, Phoebe thought that Keenan was overdoing it. Why call 911? Maybe Maysie and the kids were taking an afternoon nap.

"No." Phoebe's voice was curt.

Quickly, she texted Chief of Police Kyle Stewart on her phone. That way she didn't have to talk on the phone and alert whoever was inside the house.

It was a good thing that Kyle was a mutual friend

who attended the same church as Phoebe and Keenan. In fact, they had tried to set up a blind date between Kyle and Maysie. It hadn't worked out, but Kyle wasn't mad at them for trying.

Kyle also knew exactly what Mendenhall Retreat was about, and he often responded instantly to emergencies involving the secret hideaway that nobody in the outside world knew about.

He texted back immediately, as Phoebe had expected. If he hadn't, Phoebe would've called 911.

"Kyle is on his way," Phoebe whispered to Keenan, whose forehead was sweating in the afternoon summer heat.

Phoebe put away her phone into her quilted crossbody bag and pulled out a loaded Sig Sauer from a side compartment. The handgun had been a gift from Esperanza after Phoebe passed every level of staff training with flying colors.

Phoebe had put neither the handgun nor the training into use in the last three years, but she made sure to carry the Sig with her as a daily reminder that Esperanza had once offered her the deputy director position at Mendenhall Retreat, a position that eighty-eight-year-old Joseph Brannigan still occupied.

A slight smile crept up Keenan's lips, and a sparkle showed in his eyes.

Phoebe suspected that her husband was admiring her, but this was no time for any of that.

"Focus, darling, and lead the way." She pointed. She actually didn't know which direction they should be going, but she knew that Keenan would know what to do next.

"Yes, ma'am." Keenan's voice was all business.

CHAPTER 2

S ome things couldn't be unseen. Keenan shook all the way down to both his prosthetic legs when he pulled himself away from the single window looking into the kitchen.

"What?" Phoebe whispered, stepping in front of her husband to take a look.

Keenan pulled her back by the waist before she reached the window. He didn't want Phoebe to see the bloody mess on the floor by the kitchen table. It was clearly a crime scene, and he couldn't let Phoebe inside to contaminate it—and freak out over it.

"The door could be unlocked," Phoebe whispered as she pointed to the screen door that was ajar, stuck in that position due to the spring-loaded door closer on top of the door frame.

Keenan shook his head, mouthed "no," grabbed her free hand, and made his way back to the front of the house.

It was time for flight, not fight.

To her credit, Phoebe didn't protest as they

sprinted along the side of the house. Keenan's weapon was drawn, but Phoebe's Sig was pointed down.

They reached the driveway just as two patrol cars came up, their sirens and lights off. Chief Kyle Stewart stepped out of one of the vehicles. He seemed to walk fine today, but sometimes he'd limp a bit due to an old knee injury.

It seemed that Kyle had brought half of the Misty Mountain Police Department. Keenan guessed that the other four police officers were off duty this afternoon.

"Kyle." Panting, Keenan stopped to catch his breath as he holstered his Glock. "Blood on the front doormat, blood on the kitchen floor. Not sure if anyone's inside."

The words were out of Keenan's mouth before he realized that Phoebe was still standing next to him.

"What?" Phoebe grabbed Keenan's arm. "Jamie's in danger."

Her voice was even and calm.

That scared Keenan.

"How many people were in the house?" Kyle was taking notes on his phone. "Do you know?"

"When I left them at 6:30 this morning, there were three adults and two children," Phoebe said. "Maysie and her great-aunt, Mrs. Madison, a hired housekeeper who also cooks—Marcia, I think—and two boys aged four. Hanley and my son, Jamie."

Kyle nodded.

"I put two AirTags on Jamie. One on his backpack and the other in his right shoe." Phoebe's hands didn't shake as she swiped her phone. "Okay. I see that both items are still in the house."

"Let's start here. Give me the locations." Kyle leaned over to look at Phoebe's phone app. She took a snapshot of the map and sent it via text to Kyle's phone.

Kyle was checking the image as he asked them another question. "Has any one of you called Maysie?"

"I texted her just now. No reply." Phoebe asked if she should try again. "I could also call Mrs. Madison. As far as I know, all of them should be home. Mrs. Madison, Maysie, her son, and my son."

Kyle raised a hand to stop her from talking more. An old scar was visible across the base of his palm. "Get in your truck and back out of the driveway. Go behind the police cars and wait for me. I'll call you when I need to speak with you again. Don't go too far."

With a slight nod to Keenan, Kyle left them to talk to his officers and to call for backup.

"It's my fault." Phoebe stared at the house as she climbed into the truck. "Please, Lord, let Jamie be okay."

Keenan didn't put much stock in the AirTags because they could be removed. Jamie could've been taken out of the house without his shoes and backpack.

Keenan didn't know why his mind went that way, but his first thought was indeed that Jamie could've been abducted. Could Maysie's ex-husband have anything to do with it?

His second thought was in the form of a question. Did his current Bristol Bait project have something to do with this? If so, he could shelf it for another day, or let someone else take over.

As long as he could get Jamie back, Keenan was willing to sacrifice a promotion at Mendenhall Security.

He'd have to talk to Esperanza about bailing out of the mission. Besides, until they find Jamie, he wouldn't be going to Atlanta anytime soon. Surely Esperanza would understand that.

Keenan didn't wait for Phoebe to put on her seat belt before he backed the truck out of the driveway and onto the road as more police vehicles arrived.

The Misty Mountain Police Department didn't have a SWAT team, but all eight police officers—hand-picked former military men and women—were well trained to respond to situations that perhaps even a city police department didn't have to. This was due to the fact that even though Misty Mountain only had a thousand residents, it was twenty minutes to Mendenhall Retreat. That secret hideaway sometimes hosted unusual guests, including CIA agents, foreign diplomats, military officers, and even the Vice President of the United States, who'd brought along his entourage of medical personnel.

Therefore, Maysie Madison-Greer would be a small matter for Kyle to handle.

Kyle knew about Maysie's situation because Keenan had told him about her a while back when Phoebe insisted that Maysie could watch their son until Mendenhall Retreat finished renovating a cabin to be used as onsite childcare for staff and guests.

From the get-go, Keenan had a bad feeling about Maysie, but Phoebe wanted to help her earn some side income. It seemed like a natural fit. Maysie's four-year-old son attended the same kindergarten as Jamie. The two boys were even in the same Sunday school class at church and attended Vacation Bible School together the second week of July.

With Keenan's reluctant agreement, and based only on the relationship that Phoebe had with Maysie's great-aunt, Phoebe paid Maysie to pick up Jamie from K4 and keep him in her house until Phoebe finished work at five o'clock.

Shortly thereafter, Keenan found out about Maysie's restraining order against her ex-husband who had been in and out of jail on assault and battery charges. Right now, he was supposed to be in jail in Auburn, Alabama, because he'd beaten up his new girlfriend and made her lose an eye.

Still, Keenan understood that Phoebe didn't want to abandon her friend. After all, she was Mrs. Madison's oldest grand-niece. Mrs. Madison had been kind to Phoebe and given her a job at her funeral parlor a long time ago. She had since given up that second job to work full time for Mendenhall Retreat, but Phoebe didn't forget kindness.

And now this.

Yes, Keenan wanted to blame his wife for giving people second chances. However, he had to blame himself as well for allowing this to come to this point. He worked for Mendenhall Security that kept people safe all over the world, and yet he couldn't provide security for his own family, especially his own four-year-old son.

Keenan parked the truck in a shady spot by the side of the road under a tree with spreading branches.

"Why don't we park where we can see the house?" Phoebe asked.

"This is behind the police cars." Keenan turned off the ignition. "We need to make room for the paramedics."

As if on cue, a Sevier County Emergency Medical Service vehicle and a firetruck passed by, heading toward the Madison house.

"See?" Keenan pointed.

Phoebe started to cry as she stared at the EMS vehicle. "Is Jamie going to be okay?"

"Don't worry. God is sovereign." Keenan had heard a lot of crying, weeping, and gnashing of teeth in his line of work, both during his time in the British Special Forces as well as his years of working for Mendenhall Security. However, just one little sniffle from Phoebe sent his heart into a gut-wrenching spiral.

He reached over to squeeze Phoebe's hand, and their eyes met.

"I'm sorry." Her voice cracked.

"About what?" Keenan could make a list of all the things she should be sorry about, but he didn't. Instead, he handed her an entire tissue box.

"I should've listened to you. Maysie has too much baggage. Should've paid someone else to care for Jamie, or I could've taken him to work." Phoebe wiped her eyes.

"Mrs. Madison is there during the day as well." Then again, what could a ninety-year-old woman do if Maysie's ex-husband showed up in person? Hold him down while Maysie called the police?

"Besides, we're only twenty minutes away." It seemed that Phoebe tried to rationalize her decision.

Twenty minutes too long.

Keenan didn't want to scare her by reminding her that it wouldn't take but two seconds, not twenty minutes, to kill people. Whoever the criminal was, he or she had time to make a mess in the house.

Keenan couldn't imagine a good outcome. His finger was already pointing to Maysie's ex-husband. But wasn't he in jail in Alabama?

He texted Marie Bouchard at the Atlanta office of Mendenhall Security to ask her if Newell Greer was still in prison. The analyst was in charge of a small team of data scientists who continually processed data all day long. She would know.

When Phoebe continued to sob into a wad of soaked-through tissue, Keenan's heart broke. He prayed silently for the right words to say, and then he realized that he was also at fault.

"I should've dug deeper into Maysie's case and made a stronger point," he admitted. "I should've taken this more seriously."

Phoebe sniffled. "Next time don't hesitate to speak your mind."

"I apologize for being too busy to put enough time and effort into our family life. I left it to you most of the time." He had. Really.

"You have a lot of work to do at Mendenhall Security. I don't blame you."

"Maybe too much work."

"You can also say that I made the decision to work at the retreat office and not stay home with Jamie. If I had stayed home with him..." Phoebe straightened up. "Why would there be blood on the floor, Keenan?"

It wasn't a rhetorical question. Keenan knew that Phoebe had been trained by none other than Esperanza, the founder of Mendenhall Security and director of Mendenhall Retreat. In fact, Esperanza had personally trained every staffer. If a person didn't make it through the firearms and special operations training, they would be fired.

Phoebe didn't just pass, but she excelled at the top of the class.

Therefore, she wasn't going to ask a rhetorical question.

"Why would there be blood on the floor, Keenan?" Phoebe repeated her question.

Her voice wasn't emotional. Perhaps it had been honed by the years of her working at the Misty Mountain Funeral Home, where death and burial were a common occurrence. That past work had surely enabled Phoebe to be objective when it came to grief and the understanding of it.

Not that they were at that point yet, but Keenan felt better about how they were going to handle this going forward.

"No matter what happens, we must continue to trust God." Keenan knew he hadn't directly answered Phoebe's question, but it was because he had no idea what to tell her regarding that. The detectives and forensic pathologists would be able to shed more light on what exactly happened in the Madison kitchen.

Phoebe nodded, but she was already making another call. This time to her dad in Savannah, Georgia. Keenan listened to Phoebe's calm voice.

"No need to come here, Dad." Phoebe nodded. The phone was still at her ear. "Best thing to do is to pray for Jamie's safe return."

She did not put it on speaker, but Keenan could pretty much guess what Jerome Pendegrast said to his daughter. But the next part surprised him.

"Garrett is in town?" Phoebe looked up at Keenan and raised her eyebrows.

United States Army Special Forces officer Garrett Untermeyer was the only biological son from Phoebe's stepmother's first marriage. The Green Beret soldier rarely went home to Savannah on his time off, so this was incredible timing.

"He's coming with you to Misty Mountain?" Phoebe started to smile. "Great. We need all the help we can get to find Jamie."

She glanced over at Keenan again. He nodded in agreement. If having Phoebe's stepbrother in town made her feel better, then Keenan was all for it.

"Is Rhoda coming too?" Phoebe nodded. "Oh good. We only have two bedrooms in our cabin, but I'll check if a bigger cabin is available. What? No? Okay. I guess Breckenridge B&B is fine too. You do what you want, Dad."

It made sense to Keenan that Jerome and Rhoda wanted to stay at the B&B in town. It seemed to be a better staging area for a community search because people from Misty Mountain could attend meetings at the B&B. On the other hand, Mendenhall Retreat had strict access rules.

"Yeah, Joe Brannigan is still around. He's retiring shortly." Phoebe wiped a tear. "Yes, I think you can ask him to help organize the community search. He just turned eighty-eight, and he has a bad knee, but he's still as sharp as a tack."

Phoebe listened for a bit. Keenan couldn't hear much.

"Do you want me to send someone to pick you up at the Knoxville airport?" Phoebe finally asked. "No need? You'll get a rental car? Okay. Drive safely. Text me at every stop."

Keenan's phone rang while Phoebe was still talking to her dad.

"Sure thing. Okay. We'll be there." Keenan hung up and started the engine as he heard Phoebe say goodbye to her dad.

"Was that Kyle?" Phoebe asked.

Keenan nodded. "He wants to talk to us. I'll drive as close as we can to the entrance so we don't have to walk too far."

"Dad and Rhoda are flying in from Savannah to Knoxville," Phoebe said. "They'll get a rental car at the airport and drive here."

Knoxville, Tennessee, had the closest airport to Misty Mountain. Still, it would take an hour or so. Keenan didn't volunteer to go pick up his in-laws because he knew he'd be busy.

"Takes about three or four hours to fly to Knoxville—not including the time they wait at the airport," Phoebe said. "After they land, I'll give Dad about an hour to drive up the mountain. Longer if Rhoda drives."

Keenan nodded. In a way, he was glad that Jerome would be coming to see them. Some years ago, he'd started a community search when Phoebe left home—back in her rebellious years. Later on, Jerome also helped Iris and Camden la Salle to organize a community search to find Iris's missing sister.

Keenan parked the truck behind a police SUV, giving it enough room to back out if needed. Then he stopped Phoebe from exiting the truck.

"Let's pray first for God's help," Keenan said.

Phoebe nodded and closed her eyes.

"Take a deep breath, and I'll pray." Keenan held her hand and closed his eyes. He waited a few seconds before he prayed. "Father God, we lift up our son, Jamie, and his friend, Hanley, as well as Maysie and Mrs. Madison, and the cook, whose name has slipped my mind."

"Marcia," Phoebe whispered.

"Marcia. Okay. We don't know what happened in the house, but Lord, You know. We pray that You will keep them safe and bring them home safely to us ASAP."

Keenan paused.

"Please give Kyle and his deputies and other law enforcement officers the wisdom to solve this situation," Phoebe prayed between sobs. "Also give Dad and Rhoda a safe flight from Savannah. And keep Jamie safe, Lord."

"We know You are sovereign, Lord, and we trust that Your perfect will would prevail in this matter." Keenan dared not let his imagination wander. This was not the time to play the what-if game.

The best outcome would be to find Jamie safe and sound in the house somewhere. The house was old and had a lot of rooms and closets. Jamie knew how to play hide-and-seek, a game that Phoebe disliked because she was always afraid of not being able to find Jamie.

Keenan hated to be selfish, but at this point, he didn't care about anyone else except Phoebe and Jamie. That was to say, if Jamie was hurt in any way, Keenan knew he'd hunt down the perpetrator to the ends of the earth and kill—

Uh, bring them to justice.

"Dear Lord, help Keenan and me to operate within the law," Phoebe added in an extra prayer.

Startled, Keenan wondered why Phoebe prayed that way.

"Lord, please help us to stay strong together and work as a team. In the name of Jesus, I pray. Amen." Keenan closed out the prayer before Phoebe could say more.

"Amen!"

Keenan heard the other door slam shut before he could open his eyes.

There was Phoebe out there beyond the hood of the truck, jogging toward Kyle standing by the mailbox.

So much for staying together and working as a team.

Keenan sighed.

CHAPTER 3

To his credit, Kyle liked to keep people informed about what he was doing. That made him a great Chief of Police, well loved by the residents of Misty Mountain, but it also put him in a bad spot about things he shouldn't be making public.

This time, Phoebe absolutely wanted to know what was going on. She knew that Kyle could trust her and Keenan. In fact, if anything, they would be the ones most interested in the matter. Still, there were legal barriers if Kyle accidentally disclosed something that a judge could eventually deem inadmissible in court.

Regardless, Phoebe wasn't going to stop Kyle from talking. He was in the middle of telling her about the search warrant when Keenan joined them.

"As soon as Judge Jeong signs the search warrant and emails it back to me, my officers will reenter the house to photograph and gather the evidence." His face looked grim. "Like I said, nobody was inside in our first sweep."

"Nobody at all?" Keenan asked.

"Nobody. However, we found your son's backpack and shoes downstairs, as well as Maysie's phone upstairs."

Phoebe's knees went weak. She held on to Keenan for support, but then straightened up. This was no time to panic.

"Mrs. Madison carries her phone with her everywhere," she suddenly said. She speed-dialed the phone. "No answer. Uh-oh."

"I know her number," Kyle said. "I'll get the dispatcher to ping her phone."

Keenan looked toward the house.

Phoebe followed his gaze. She pointed at the empty garage. "Maysie's van is gone."

"I noticed that too." Kyle went on to explain how they would search for the five missing people, assuring them that they would use both physical and digital assets available to them.

"Like what?" Phoebe asked.

"Like street cameras in town, talking to the neighbors to see if they saw anything."

"My dad is coming in the morning, and he can help with a community search," Phoebe said.

"As long as he's not in our way."

"Gotcha." Phoebe figured that Kyle had said that because he had never met Dad. Dad wouldn't get in the way. If anything, he'd be helpful.

"We will also check the DMV about Maysie's van. Mrs. Madison doesn't have a car, does she?"

Phoebe shook her head. "She hasn't driven in twenty years."

"I need both of you to go downtown so we can

record an interview with you," Kyle said. "Once we have all the information about the two boys, we'll send out an AMBER Alert."

Phoebe had seen those America's Missing: Broadcast Emergency Response alerts on electronic message signs over highways. Never once had she thought that it could come this close to home.

"I took a photo of Jamie before we left our cabin this morning," Phoebe said.

"Good. We can use that."

"I don't know if April has photos of her sister and nephew," Phoebe added. "She was just here yesterday afternoon visiting Maysie when I picked up Jamie. She was telling me about taking a trip to visit her other sister, June."

Keenan chuckled a bit but then caught himself. "I didn't mean to take it lightly, but I always thought it was interesting that the Madison sisters are named April, Maysie, and June."

Phoebe was a bit annoyed that her husband could joke at a time like this. Then again, he had undergone enormous dangers and lived through them all, so perhaps humor was a survival tactic as well.

Phoebe turned to Kyle, who was checking his phone. "Are you going to ask the forest rangers for help?"

"We'll send the information to the National Park Service rangers since they run the Great Smoky Mountains, just so they can be on the lookout."

"The forest would be a great place to hide these kids—but a terrible one too because it would be hard to find them." Keenan looked at his wife warily.

"Not with drones." A thousand things spun

through Phoebe's mind. "I think we need to call Espy and ask for resources that Mendenhall Security can provide."

Keenan nodded.

Kyle looked up from his phone. "Okay. Judge Jeong has signed the search warrant. So we're going back in. Would you please go to the station yourself? I will let Zell know that you're on the way. The sooner he interviews you, the sooner the search can begin in earnest."

In a small town like Misty Mountain, everyone knew who Detective Zell Benson was. In fact, he had been coaching middle school summer football camp every year for the past nineteen years. In his sixties, he'd been married to the same woman for forty years, and they were blessed with three kids and five grandchildren.

Phoebe had thought that the next time Dad came to town, she'd introduce him to Zell. They would get along with their shared interest in college football, although Dad was a Georgia Bulldogs fan while Zell was all for the Tennessee Volunteers.

"Thank you." Phoebe wanted to add that she would be praying for Kyle, but he was gone.

"I was going to ask him about Maysie's ex." Keenan sighed. "Maybe we'll just tell Zell when we see him at the MMPD."

Half an hour later, while Phoebe and Keenan were at the MMPD headquarters on Main Street, word came that Mrs. Madison had been found five miles away, passed out in Maysie's van.

In the same van, they had also found Marcia breathing erratically and bleeding profusely from stab wounds in her stomach and legs. The paramedics worked on her for over twenty minutes, but she suffered a cardiac arrest and passed away in the ambulance.

Before Detective Zell Benson could finish the interview with Phoebe and Keenan, word came that Mrs. Madison had regained consciousness in the emergency room and asked to see Phoebe.

Zell drove Keenan and Phoebe to the hospital roughly five minutes west on Main Street. They met Kyle at the nurse's station and left Zell there to chat with Kyle. Phoebe wanted to see Mrs. Madison right away, and Keenan accompanied her.

They found Mrs. Madison in a private room with a view of the hospital parking lot. Unfortunately, the poor woman, all wrinkled and pale, was in and out of consciousness.

She had a fever, and the doctors had been trying to bring it down. It turned out that she had been sick with a sinus infection for days, and no one had known because she'd refused to see the doctor.

"She was in her room upstairs most of the time. The kids were in the basement. Maybe that's why the kids were fine and didn't catch her cold or whatever this was." Phoebe sat down on the edge of the couch closest to the hospital bed.

Mrs. Madison was asleep now, and they'd have to wait for her to wake up to talk to her. The nurses left the room.

Before Phoebe could chat with Keenan, Kyle and Zell walked into the room. Kyle found a spot on the other side of Keenan. Zell found a chair by the sink, carried it to the foot of the bed, and sat down.

"Ac...accent." Mrs. Madison muttered. Her eyes were still closed.

"What?" Phoebe leaned toward her. "Accent?"

Mrs. Madison nodded.

"Which accent?" Phoebe asked.

"Eu...European."

Phoebe glanced at Keenan. She knew that Keenan was in a couple of classified projects in Europe, but he hadn't been able to tell her a thing due to the nature of the mission.

"Mrs. Madison, can you tell us more?" Zell came up to the other side of the bed. He held a recorder in his hand.

Mrs. Madison mumbled something that sounded like "shh" or "slush." After she repeated it a few times, Phoebe got it.

Scottish.

"Who has a Scottish accent?" Phoebe asked.

Nobody suggested Maysie's ex-husband, and it seemed that the MMPD officers didn't want to plant ideas in Mrs. Madison's mind.

"Who?" Phoebe asked again.

"The woman."

"Where did you see this woman?" Kyle asked.

Mrs. Madison didn't reply right away.

"At the house?" Phoebe asked.

Mrs. Madison shook her head. She took a deep breath.

Silence fell in the room. Everyone waited for Mrs. Madison to speak again.

"Ne...Newell."

"Newell Greer?" Zell asked.

Maysie's ex-husband.

Phoebe staggered back. She regretted it whole-heartedly now. She should never have left Jamie with Maysie. Even though Phoebe and Maysie were friends in the women's group at church, it didn't mean that Phoebe had to leave Jamie in Maysie's care just to help the single mother earn some extra income.

Phoebe could have helped Maysie in another way instead of risking the life of her own child.

She blinked.

Keenan wrapped his arm around Phoebe's waist. His arm was warm, but it didn't help at all.

Wracked with guilt, Phoebe didn't know what to do. She couldn't even pray. No words formed in her mind.

Mrs. Madison nodded. "Called her."

"Call her? Or called her?" Phoebe asked.

"Called."

"So Newell Greer called a woman with a Scottish accent," Kyle said.

Mrs. Madison pointed an arthritic finger at Kyle. "Bingo."

"When and where did he call her?" Zell asked.

"In the van."

"How did Newell get y'all into the van?" Kyle asked.

"He didn't, that coward. His loaded Smith & Wesson M&P M2.0 did." Her sharp voice startled everyone.

How could this soft-spoken owner of the Misty Mountain Funeral Home who wouldn't hurt a fly suddenly know about the weapon in Newell's hand?

"Are you sure?" Kyle asked.

"It was the same handgun that my poor Cecil

gave his father a long time ago, back when his father worked as an embalmer at the funeral home."

Cecil Madison had always been "poor Cecil" since he passed away of heart failure while conducting a funeral at the parlor some thirty or forty years ago. Mrs. Madison never remarried.

Mrs. Madison's eyes turned toward Phoebe. Slowly, she lifted her frail hand toward her. "I'm sorry."

Phoebe held her cold hand in hers. "Don't worry. God is sovereign."

Mrs. Madison had tears in her eyes. "They should've taken me instead of the boys."

Wow. Eight words.

She must be regaining her strength. Either that or the antibiotics and intravenous fluids had kicked in.

"Pray?" Mrs. Madison squeezed Phoebe's hands.

Any closer and she would probably catch Mrs. Madison's cold. Now Phoebe wished she had worn a mask to block out the potentially airborne fluids.

Mrs. Madison coughed and cleared her throat.

If I perish, I perish...

"Yes, let's pray." Phoebe closed her eyes and waited.

They all waited.

Nobody said a word.

So Phoebe did. "Dear Lord Jesus, we come before You now to pray for the safe return of Jamie, Hanley, and Maysie. We have no idea where they are, but You do. We ask that You give them the fortitude to endure, patience to wait for rescue, and faith to know that You are with them. In the strong and mighty name of Jesus, I pray. Amen."

"Amen." Mrs. Madison opened her eyes again. "Newell gets paid in cash."

"Got it." Zell glanced at Kyle, who nodded.

"We'll do everything to find your son, okay?" Kyle tapped his phone.

"How can we help?" Keenan said.

Phoebe realized that he hadn't spoken much since Mrs. Madison said the word "Scottish." Maybe that triggered something. Rang a bell?

"Go home and wait," Kyle said. "We'll stay with Mrs. Madison a while longer to see if we can get more information."

"You'll be talking to Newell Greer?"

"We'll be talking to many people." It was all Kyle would tell Keenan.

"Mendenhall Security can help in a big way," Keenan said. "I'll talk to Espy."

"For data, you'd think we would call Binary Systems instead." Zell looked up from his phone notepad.

"Yes, but Binary Systems deals with the digital realm," Keenan said. "You have eight officers at MMPD. Mendenhall Security has two hundred worldwide. If we're dealing with a Scottish mastermind, then you need all the help you can get."

Scottish mastermind?

Phoebe was almost sure that Keenan knew something he wasn't telling her or the MMPD. Something that surely Esperanza also knew, considering that she was Keenan's boss at Mendenhall Security.

Phoebe also realized that the sooner she secured the deputy director position at Mendenhall Retreat, the sooner she'd get clearance to access the toolset that could help her find and rescue Jamie.

Assuming the boy was still alive.

Tears formed in her eyes, but she held them back. She had to hold her emotions in check or else she wouldn't be able to handle this crisis.

Lord, help me look at this situation from Your perspective, not mine. I can't see anything. There's a thick fog in front of me.

For some reason, Romans 12:2 popped into her head, reminding her that she had to renew her mind if she wanted a fresh viewpoint on the situation.

> *And do not be conformed to this world, but be transformed by the renewing of your mind, that you may prove what is that good and acceptable and perfect will of God.*

She felt the presence of the Lord in her heart and knew that everything was going to be okay.

No matter the outcome.

That was hard to digest.

Of course, I want Jamie home safely.

However, Phoebe knew she had to trust God for everything. Now wasn't the time for her to rely on her nine years of training under Esperanza, although that had enabled her to be strong for such a time as this. Even that strength had come from God, as it was written in Psalm 29:11.

> *The Lord will give strength to His people;*
> *The Lord will bless His people with peace.*

"Couldn't I just call the FBI instead of you?" Kyle asked.

Phoebe wasn't sure if Kyle was jesting, but this was no time for jokes.

"Whatever, friend. Just know that I'll clear this with Espy, and we'll be ready to help in any way we can."

Keenan's voice was deliberately low, but Phoebe could sense fear in him. He feared losing his son.

Silently, Phoebe prayed Isaiah 41:10 for her husband, and continued to pray all the way back to the MMPD station, where Zell dropped them off in front of their pickup truck.

On the way back to their cabin at Mendenhall Retreat, Phoebe read Isaiah 41:10 aloud to him.

> *Fear not, for I am with you;*
>> *Be not dismayed, for I am your God.*
>> *I will strengthen you,*
>> *Yes, I will help you,*
>> *I will uphold you with My righteous right*
> *hand.*

Keenan nodded. "Thank you for reminding me to trust God for Jamie...and for you."

"And you too," Phoebe said.

When they arrived at their cabin, Keenan parked the pickup. "I'm going to drop you off and go back to my office. I need to make some calls. I'm going to cancel my trip to Atlanta, but I have to let Espy know."

"Can you call from your home office?" Phoebe wasn't trying to tell him what to do, but they each had their own home offices so that they could sometimes work from home, even though Mendenhall Lodge was only a five-minute drive away in a golf cart.

"I suppose I could too." Keenan set the brakes and got out of the pickup truck. "I'm famished."

As they walked toward their cabin's front door, Phoebe realized that she hadn't cooked any dinner nor did they have any leftovers. "How about we eat at the lodge tonight?"

"Sure."

Keenan didn't sweat the small stuff like meals and such. He wasn't a picky eater, and he'd eat anything as long as there was meat.

"I wonder what's on the menu." Phoebe swiped her phone to check the lodge app.

Keenan didn't say anything as he unlocked the door, unset the alarm, and made his way toward his home office. He shut the door.

Phoebe didn't hear a clicking sound, so she knew that Keenan hadn't locked the office door. That was to say, he wanted some privacy and alone time, but he didn't mean to shut her out.

Fair enough.

Phoebe had her own thing to deal with too. Firstly, she had no access to the MMPD. What were they working on now? For one, Newell Greer had moved up from being a person of interest to a suspect. If his fingerprints were found inside the Madison house, then the case against him strengthened.

What happened inside that house?

Without access to MMPD case files or Mendenhall Security associates, Phoebe was a mere civilian standing outside the window, looking in, but unable to participate.

But...

She had contacts of her own. She texted Maysie's sister, April, who used to be Mrs. Madison's full-time caregiver until she married and moved to be closer to the Misty Mountain College campus where her husband was the dean of the art department.

April texted back almost right away.

APRIL

I'm at the hospital with Aunt Winnie.

PHOEBE

How long will you be there?

APRIL

Visiting hours end at nine o'clock.

PHOEBE

I was there earlier, but I want to go back to see you after dinner.

APRIL

You mean to see Aunt Winnie?

PHOEBE

No, you. I have questions for you.

APRIL

Come on over. I'm here until nine.

PHOEBE

I can bring desserts from the Mendenhall Lodge kitchen.

APRIL

Oooh. Bring anything. LOL.

Phoebe went to the kitchen to get something to drink. There were a couple of bottles of sparkling water left in the refrigerator. She leaned against the sink and drank them straight up. The carbonated fizzle went down her throat the wrong way, and she coughed.

"Hopefully it's just water and I'm not catching Mrs. Madison's cold," Phoebe said aloud.

"Catch what?" Keenan's voice came from the door to the kitchen.

Phoebe had no idea how long he'd been standing there.

"Mrs. Madison is sick." Phoebe screwed the cap back on the glass water bottle and put it down on the counter. "I don't want to catch it."

"Then have you washed your hands since you left the hospital?"

"Oh, good point." Phoebe turned around and washed her hands in the kitchen sink.

Keenan came up behind her and wove his arms around her waist. He placed his chin on her shoulder. "I love you so much."

"Enough to tell me the whole truth and nothing but the truth?" Phoebe dried her hands on a clean dish towel.

Keenan seemed to be surprised by the question. He didn't answer her right away, which meant that he was trying to figure out how to respond to her in a non-suspicious and non-confrontational way.

Phoebe was looking for transparency, and she wasn't sure she was going to get it tonight.

"We'll have to take two cars to the lodge," Keenan said. "Espy has called an emergency meeting at seven o'clock. I need a secure channel, which is at my office at the lodge."

Seven o'clock. That worked out. It was almost six now. If they ate for half an hour, Phoebe could drive to the hospital and be there by seven o'clock. Then she'd have two hours to chat with April and be there in case Mrs. Madison remembered more things from her harrowing experience of being abducted.

Phoebe nodded. "How long is the meeting?"

"Not sure. You know Espy. Her meetings vary. Sometimes they're short. Sometimes they're long. Never know with her."

"Say two hours, give or take." Phoebe had worked with Esperanza long enough to be able to average her meeting times.

"So we have to go now if we want to have an hour to eat."

"I wish Jamie was here. He loves the breaded shrimp at the lodge." Phoebe's voice cracked.

"And the fries. He eats too many fries. But then, he's a growing boy. When he comes home, I won't complain about the fries anymore." Keenan almost kept talking.

Phoebe wondered what was on his mind. Was he trying to keep talking to distract her from the agony of waiting for news?

"They use beef tallow to cook the fries, so it's healthy," Phoebe added.

Keenan stared at her, then pulled her close. Gently, he kissed her forehead, then her cheeks, and then the tip of her nose.

He drew her closer, his warm breath on her face.

"If I didn't have to go to work tonight..." he said in almost a whisper. Then he kissed her on the lips, pouring his desire into that one act.

Pulling away, his eyelids half-closed, he said, "I wish I could tell you everything, but I can't. Even if I could, I don't want you to worry."

Was that his answer to her question earlier about telling her the truth in its entirety?

"The truth shall set you free." Phoebe hoped it didn't sound like a reprimand, even though she had quoted John 8:32.

And you shall know the truth, and the truth shall make you free.

"Don't stay up to wait for me." Keenan switched back to work mode. "I'll be very late. Since I can't be in Atlanta in person, I have to hand my role over to someone else who is already on the ground."

"I'm sure it will all work out. Espy understands that you need to be here to look for your abducted son."

Yes, abducted.

Phoebe was sure of it.

Keenan's phone rang.

"Whassup, Espy?" He glanced at his wife. "Now? I was going to dinner with my wife. All right. I'll tell her."

Phoebe had almost expected it. "Let me guess. The meeting's been pushed forward by two hours."

"Close. I have to get there now." Keenan frowned. "New operatives need handholding."

"Training, you mean."

"You can drop me off and go for dinner yourself. I'll eat afterwards."

"I don't know if I have any appetite, truth be told."

Keenan grinned. "I'm going to miss dinner with you."

"Does it even matter right now?" Phoebe wasn't angry, just a little frustrated. "Jamie is missing."

Keenan nodded. He had nothing to say.

Neither had Phoebe, as she let him go.

CHAPTER 4

Homemade apple pie in hand, Phoebe arrived at Mrs. Madison's hospital room to find the latter fast asleep and snoring gently.

April Moreno, nee Madison, was five months pregnant and sitting on the couch looking at her tablet computer. She smiled at Phoebe and eyed the apple pie floating toward her.

"A whole pie?" Her eyes grew big as she whispered.

"For you and your husband, even though he's a chef and all. But he's not a baker, so this should be a gift he wouldn't mind, would he?"

"Nah." April shook her head. "He's mainly teaching these days, so if someone else bakes for him, he's happy if I'm happy. Right now, I'm delighted."

"I brought some plates and knives and forks." Phoebe lifted a tote bag in her other hand.

"So thoughtful. Thank you." April's voice trembled. "I'm so sorry about Jamie. I'm so sorry."

"Your sister and your nephew were also taken, so it's bad for both of our families."

"I've already watched the videos, and so has Kyle. I don't know how Maysie could've married such a loser. Even after the divorce, he was still after her—restraining order notwithstanding."

"Life is hard."

"I know." April handed the tablet to Phoebe. "I've logged into the surveillance system. You look at whatever you need while I eat some pie."

"Okay."

"I told the surveillance company to give the MMPD whatever they need, but for you, my friend, I've logged in under my own account."

April went to wash her hands while Phoebe pieced together the sequence of events.

It wasn't easy to watch. In sequential order, the videos showed that Marcia had opened the door for Newell and his girlfriend while Maysie was in the shower, and the two kids were watching cartoons in the den. Mrs. Madison was in the kitchen making herself an afternoon snack. As soon as Newell pulled out a gun, it all went downhill from there.

Somehow, Newell had managed to round up five people into Maysie's van in the garage. Marcia had gunshot wounds. Maysie and Mrs. Madison looked visibly shaken and scared.

The two kids were blindfolded with their mouths taped and hands tied behind their backs. Wrapped in blankets, they were carried by Newell out of the house.

Phoebe's emotions ricocheted between anger and fear as she watched the videos several times, each time wondering if she missed anything critical to the case.

Before she realized it, visiting hours were over. A night nurse came to check on Mrs. Madison and reminded them that they had to leave.

"I'll come back tomorrow," April told the nurse.

"I'll need some help with studying these videos." Phoebe didn't want to ask for more than April could give her.

"Tell you what." April thought for a second. "The security firm doesn't like access from other accounts, so how about you keep my tablet overnight? Is that enough time?"

"I'd better write down your PIN to the tablet and the password to the surveillance server." Phoebe found a napkin and jotted them down as April gave them to her.

They packed up the remainder of the apple pie so that April could take it home with her. They left the plate, fork, and napkins in the hospital room because April thought she could use them the next day when she visited.

"Thank you very much." Phoebe hugged April as gently as she could around her belly. "You drive home safely, okay?"

April nodded. "I'll be praying. You don't worry about Aunt Winnie. I'll take care of her here."

"Don't wear yourself out."

"I won't. Don't worry, and take care."

They parted ways at the brightly lit hospital parking lot, not worried at all about their safety because the hospital had guards patrolling the property, and the police station was nearby.

However, the only reason this hospital existed was primarily to serve Mendenhall Retreat guests. As a result, the residents of Misty Mountain also benefited. The guards were there to keep nosy paparazzi and crime reporters from walking into the hospital, looking for rumored patients.

Once Phoebe drove away from the hospital, she no longer felt safe. Then again, she could sense how small her faith was at a moment like this. She wondered if it was even smaller than the mustard seed that the Lord spoke about in Matthew 17:19-20 after He had cured a child of demonic possession.

> *Then the disciples came to Jesus privately and said, "Why could we not cast it out?"*
>
> *So Jesus said to them, "Because of your unbelief; for assuredly, I say to you, if you have faith as a mustard seed, you will say to this mountain, 'Move from here to there,' and it will move; and nothing will be impossible for you."*

Phoebe cried quietly on the drive from the hospital to Joe Brannigan's house. Parked outside his house, she called him. He picked up on the second ring.

"Hey, Phoebe, I already talked with your dad," Joe said right away. "Once he gets here, we'll organize our search. We'll be based at the Breckenridge B&B because they promised to provide free meals for us."

"Thank you." Phoebe felt better as she listened to Joe's calm, grandfatherly voice.

Over the last several years, Joe had been a pillar of strength at the retreat, often acting as a lay Christian counselor for guests who needed someone to talk to confidentially about their problems or traumatic experiences.

Once Joe retired, his many hats would all retire with him. It was clear to Phoebe that Mendenhall Retreat needed a chaplain. Whether she ended up as the deputy director or not, she would ask Esperanza to prayerfully consider such a full-time position.

"Don't be afraid," Joe continued.

"Do I look afraid?" Phoebe was surprised at his words.

"If you're not afraid, you're not human. It's only natural for us to be afraid," Joe continued. "However, as Christians, it's supernatural not to be afraid because we have the Lord."

Joe went on to share Psalm 27:1 with Phoebe. She listened over the phone as he read the words.

The Lord is my light and my salvation;
Whom shall I fear?
The Lord is the strength of my life;
Of whom shall I be afraid?

"Thank you for reminding me that the Lord is my light to find Jamie," Phoebe said.

"In Christ there is no darkness at all." Joe went on to read 1 John 1:5 aloud, like he was shouting or something.

This is the message which we have heard from Him
and declare to you, that God is light and in Him is
no darkness at all.

"We know what salvation means," Joe said. "Phoebe, you are saved because you believed in Jesus Christ for the forgiveness of your sins. Now you belong to the Lord. He is your light and your salvation."

"Amen."

"The last part of Psalm 27:1 says that the Lord is also your strength," Joe reminded her. "If the Lord is your salvation and strength, you should fear no one."

Sitting in her truck, Phoebe nodded. She was also thinking about the ramifications of the statement for someone such as Joe, a former soldier who had to take the fight to the enemies and who might not have returned unscathed. The fact that he had lived this long was a testimony to his bravery, and that bravery was due to Christ.

Help me to be brave, Lord.

"Now pull your truck in my driveway and come inside while I make us a pot of tea," Joe said. "It's going to be a long night."

"Wait. How did you know I'm outside your house?" Phoebe looked around.

It was dark all around her outside the truck.

"I have security cameras everywhere." Joe chuckled. "You can't hide in the bushes, young lady."

"I wasn't hiding in the bushes. I'm sitting in my pickup truck."

"Figure of speech. Figure of speech." Then he paused. "Are you coming in or not? I've got to lock the door after you."

"On my way." Phoebe parked the truck outside the closed garage door. Before she could get out, the garage door opened.

Dressed like he was ready to go to work, Joe ambled through his tidy garage, walking past his flashy-red Porsche 718 Cayman that he drove to work on most days.

He used to own two Harleys, but he'd sold them years ago after his wife had disapproved of them. It had been her deathbed wish for him to stay away from motorcycles and other two-wheelers—she'd made sure to get all grounds covered—and live long enough to walk their daughter down the aisle.

Phoebe got out of her truck with her purse and April's tablet.

"Only family and close friends come in through the garage." Joe ushered her into his house.

After a brief explanation of the events of the day, Phoebe was ready to show Joe the tablet.

"Let's go to the kitchen table." Joe led the way.

They sat down at the farmhouse table. Phoebe sat next to Joe so that they could both watch the tablet together.

After they did, Joe opened his laptop.

"Everything that happens from now onward is top secret," Joe said.

"Yes, sir."

At first, Joe used his Mendenhall Retreat clearance to video-call Iseul Kim at Binary Systems in Atlanta to help them track down Newell Greer based on the conversation he had with Maysie inside the house. The conversation pointed to the fact that Newell lived within driving distance of Misty Mountain. He wanted to reconcile with Maysie while keeping his current girlfriend. That threw the latter into a tirade, and they argued.

The argument yielded a treasure trove of information, including the fact that Newell worked as a part-time farmhand on a pig farm twenty miles outside Gatlinburg.

"Hmm..." Joe rubbed his chin. "I think we need to go to the pig farm."

"Now?" Phoebe was stunned.

"Pack up." Joe turned toward his laptop where the video call with Iseul was live. "Could you tell me the exact address of the barn?"

"It's off the road, but I can give you the coordinates," Iseul said.

"Good enough. We'll be in touch." Joe cracked his knuckles.

Phoebe's hands started to shake.

"Remember what I told you? Don't be afraid." Joe got out of his chair with difficulty, holding on to the dining table with one hand and the backrest of the chair with the other.

Phoebe wondered if she should help him, but he didn't need any help once he straightened up.

"My knees are killing me," Joe complained. "Anyway, I have to pack a few things, and then we're out of here, all right? You drive your truck. I'm not getting my Porsche dirty at a pig farm."

Phoebe didn't want to watch April's videos another time, so she checked her phone. Well, it was out of battery. On the kitchen countertop was a charger cable that fit her phone, so she plugged it in and charged it up while waiting for Joe to get going.

Soon, she heard Joe coming down the hallway, his cell phone to his ear. "You do whatever you need to do, Iseul, and so will I."

Wearing a jacket, he looked puffed up somewhat. Phoebe wondered what he'd packed into the pockets of the jacket.

Joe hung up the phone, grunted, and turned to Phoebe. "Let's go. Got the key?"

Phoebe fished for it in her purse.

Joe's phone rang, and he answered it. It was his daughter, Jessica. "Nice of you to call me to say good night. When do you fly out? I see. So I won't see you for a few more days?" He paused and listened. "Me? Busy doing things. Right now, I'm helping Phoebe. Yeah, she's here. You want to talk to her?"

Joe handed Phoebe the phone, but motioned for her to keep walking. They exited the garage as Phoebe updated Jessica on the situation. In other words, she had nothing new to say. Jamie was still missing.

"Thank you for your prayers. Have a good night." Phoebe barely finished talking when Joe took the phone back from her.

Phoebe unlocked the truck doors, and they climbed in.

"Can we pray before we go?" Phoebe asked.

"Always." Joe didn't wait for Phoebe to pray. He dove into a power warrior's prayer that sounded like he had asked God to send down all the angels in heaven to sweep across the land to find little James O'Tierney.

Before Phoebe could cry, Joe instructed her to drive.

From Misty Mountain to the pig farm outside Gatlinburg, they hardly said a word except when Joe thought Phoebe was going to drive off the road. She wasn't. She just didn't want to drive over a box turtle trying to cross the two-lane country road, for example.

Closer to the pig farm, the sky was still cloudy, but here and there, a partial moon shone through.

Phoebe recalled the times when Jamie had sat with her on the porch swing as they watched a full moon in the evening sky. She recalled what she'd said to her son.

No matter where we go around the world, we're looking at the same moon.

She wondered if Jamie had an opportunity to be outside at night. If he looked up at the sky, would he remember that this was the same moon that God had hung in the sky? Would he remember that his mommy would also see the same moon?

Then perhaps he'd remember Genesis 1:16 that Phoebe had read to him every time they looked at the moon.

Then God made two great lights: the greater light
to rule the day, and the lesser light to rule the night.
He made the stars also.

If Jamie could remember God, then he might not be afraid.

Phoebe made a mental note to continue to teach Jamie not to be afraid, just as Joe had taught Phoebe tonight.

Phoebe thanked God for Joe, whom God had brought into her life when she needed a grandfatherly figure. In fact, God had given her a whole family, from her adopted parents and sister to her step-brothers and stepsister, as well as people at work such as the grandfatherly Joe and sisterly Esperanza.

And then God brought Keenan into her life. And now Jamie.

If these people had all been the Lord's gift to her, then wouldn't He also protect them all?

Checking his phone to see Iseul's messages, Joe pointed ahead of them. "Newell Greer's phone is in that barn."

"What barn?" Phoebe tried not to drive too fast on the unpaved road that made the truck bounce. It was all dark around them except for her headlights.

She flashed on the brightest headlights the truck had.

And saw the barn.

The rundown structure with tall weeds all around it wasn't exactly inside the pig farm fence. That made it easier for them to access, and less likely to be arrested for trespassing.

"I'm turning off the headlights now," Phoebe said.

"Just don't hit anything."

Phoebe pointed to the sky. "God's moon will light the way."

The truck rumbled on the dirt road. Phoebe kept the speed at ten miles per hour, not wanting the engine noise to attract attention.

She coasted to a stop just outside the closed door of the barn. Before she could unbuckle her seat belt, Joe was already outside the pickup truck, his Sig Sauer drawn, as he inched toward the barn.

Realizing she was unarmed, Phoebe wasn't sure what she was supposed to do. She looked for her purse, and then realized she probably shouldn't take her purse with her to a showdown in the big barn.

She reached over to the glove compartment. Sure enough, Keenan had left a Glock there. It was loaded.

Phoebe jumped out of the truck and went after Joe to provide rear cover for him.

Before they arrived at the barn door, it creaked open.

Joe and Phoebe hid in the shadows of a bush.

Someone's head popped out, looking to the left and right. He was about to close the door, when Joe lurched forward like the wind.

He pushed the barn door in, as though he was a linebacker pushing against a blocking sled at the practice field. Then he tackled the man at the door and pinned him to the barn floor.

A dim portable lantern hanging on a hook about five feet above the ground provided enough lighting on the barn floor covered with hay, which was now all over the man.

Newell Greer.

He hadn't changed clothes from what he'd worn at Mrs. Madison's house. Other than the video and the occasional photos that Maysie had shown her, Phoebe had never actually met the person.

Joe put a knee on the man's chest and pressed his Sig in his face. "Newell Greer, your time is up."

"Grandpa, I don't even know you." Newell was out of breath.

"Don't you *grandpa* me." Joe pistol-whipped Newell's face until his nose was bloody.

Uh-oh.

"I'll look for some ropes," Phoebe said to Joe.

As she was searching, she heard a moan and then silence.

"Maysie?" Phoebe walked toward the noise.

There was no more sound coming from the pile of hay, but Phoebe dug with her hands. Then she spotted a spading fork nearby and used that instead of her hands. She tried to be careful with it just in case she impaled the person who had produced the single moan.

In short order, she lifted up enough hay to reveal two legs tied together at the ankles.

Phoebe dropped the fork and pushed away the hay until the entire person was revealed.

"Maysie! I found you." Phoebe nearly cried. "Thank You, Jesus."

Maysie did not respond.

Phoebe checked her pulse. It was there. "Maysie, wake up! Please don't die."

She was dressed in a nightgown that covered only down to her mid-thigh. She had bruises and cuts all over her body. Her wrists were also tied.

Phoebe couldn't begin to imagine what might have happened to her.

Best not to think about that.

She'd let the law enforcement sort it out later.

Right now, Phoebe wanted to keep Maysie alive for the sake of her own son.

As a staff member of Mendenhall Retreat, Phoebe was trained in first aid, but Maysie seemed to be seriously injured, considering the multiple bruises and lacerations on her head. The bleeding had stopped, but Phoebe was afraid to move her. With head injuries, any movement could be bad.

However, she had to get her to a recovery position on her side. How could she do that safely without causing her brain more injuries?

Phoebe reached into her pocket to get her phone, but realized that she didn't have her phone with her. Oh, she had left it charging in Joe's kitchen.

Phoebe walked back to borrow Joe's phone, only to find that he had found some ropes by himself and had tied up Newell in so many different knots—including multiple bowline knots— that Newell wasn't going to unravel himself.

Joe walked past Phoebe with a bucket of dirty water.

"I found Maysie. She's passed out." Phoebe said to him quietly. "We need to call 911, but I left my phone at your house."

Joe put down the bucket of water, retrieved his phone, swiped it, and gave it to Phoebe. "Call now before I wake him up."

Phoebe called 911 and gave them the coordinates of the barn. "We found one of the abducted victims, Maysie. She's breathing, but she's unconscious with head injuries. What should I do? I'm afraid to move her."

The dispatcher told her several things she had to do to keep Maysie's airway open and how to put her in a safe recovery position. Even though Phoebe had some training back at the retreat, no one there had ever been passed out in front of her.

Dead, yes, but unconscious, no.

Thus, it was good to hear the dispatcher walk her through it so that she didn't miss any steps.

Phoebe had to stay with Maysie to check her breathing every minute.

After Phoebe hung up, she heard a heavy dragging noise. She saw Joe pulling Newell toward her.

Joe would surely have heard Phoebe talking to the dispatcher.

"We might not have enough time between now and when the paramedics arrive," Joe said.

"To do what?" Phoebe snapped a few photos of Maysie. Perhaps the prosecutors could use them in court. She took a few more photos from all angles for good measure.

Joe grunted. Apparently, he either didn't know or didn't want to tell her outright.

"The nearest fire station is twenty minutes out. Is that enough time for you?" Phoebe asked.

Joe nodded.

"How were you able to look for the ropes?" Phoebe eyed the unconscious Newell.

"I tasered him first. He passed out on his own." Joe dumped the bucket of dirty water on Newell's face.

Newell woke up.

"What did you do to Maysie?" Phoebe asked.

"She tried to run."

"So you hit her repeatedly until she passed out? She could've died, and you'd be a murderer."

"She's alive, isn't she?"

"No thanks to you."

Joe stepped in. "Where's your girlfriend?" Phoebe asked.

"She left me." Newell went into an expletive tirade.

"Watch your mouth," Joe snapped. "There are two ladies in the room."

At Mendenhall Retreat, Phoebe had heard them all. Even though she was a Christian, not everyone else was Christian. Some of the Christians cussed at times, but Phoebe didn't because she wanted to set a clean example for Jamie.

"Where's my son?" Phoebe stepped forward.

"You're Jamie's mother?" Newell's face went pale, and he seemed to be scared to death.

At first Phoebe thought he was scared of her, but not. She glanced to her left and saw Joe pointing not one, but two Sig Sauer handguns, at his manhood.

The no-nonsense eighty-eight-year-old former soldier's finger was steady on the trigger. "One shot or two? He'll still live and can still talk, but he won't be able to reproduce henceforth. I might also take out a hip, or two. I won't know until I try. Ready?"

"No! Please...! No!" Newell's cowardly voice filled the air.

"Then talk." Joe didn't move his weapons.

"She paid me." Newell's teeth chattered. "Said she was calling from Scotland."

Which could be false either way.

As far as Phoebe knew, many of Keenan's and Esperanza's former associates could put on a pretty good accent and fool a few people.

"Check my phone," Newell said. "She texted me just now."

"Where's your phone?"

"Back pocket."

Joe looked at Phoebe as though it was her job to get the phone from Newell's back pocket.

He was all tied up, so he couldn't make a run for it. It should be all right. Phoebe pushed at his body with her boot until he was on his side. She retrieved the phone.

She wished she had worn gloves because now her fingerprints were all over the phone, along with Newell's.

"PIN?" His personal identification number would unlock the phone.

Newell gave it.

On the phone were phone messages from Newell's client, a woman named "Angel." It might be a person disguised as this particular woman by using a real-time voice modulation software to change his or her voice.

"That's her," Newell said. "She called herself 'Angel.' That's all I know."

One text message session made the hair on Phoebe's neck rise. With Joe's phone, she took snapshots of the text messages.

ANGEL

He will pay.

NEWELL

For what?

ANGEL

He knows. That's enough.

NEWELL

Is this an ex-boyfriend?

ANGEL

No.

> **NEWELL**
>
> Is this a vendetta?

ANGEL

Maybe. We were colleagues. I
thought he was my friend.

> **NEWELL**
>
> He hurts you. You hurt him back.
> Something like that?

ANGEL

He made my husband leave me. So
now I make his son leave him.

> **NEWELL**
>
> Do unto others and all that?

ANGEL

Something like that.

> **NEWELL**
>
> If it's tit for tat, wouldn't it make more
> sense to take his wife instead of
> his son?

ANGEL

Shut up.

Firstly, "Angel" had identified herself as someone who had worked with the father of the child she had abducted. Since Keenan's son was abducted, it made sense that Keenan was the man with whom "Angel" was angry.

Secondly, Phoebe wasn't sure whether to feel slighted that "Angel" hadn't considered her more important to Keenan than their son. The lack of logic —perhaps due to the years of unresolved anger making "Angel" go sideways—might just be the blessing in disguise that Phoebe needed.

Thirdly, all this told Phoebe that Keenan might have already known who had abducted their son. Why wouldn't he have told Phoebe then? Why would Keenan hide secrets from her? Was it due to the security clearance at Mendenhall Security? Then Keenan could have asked Esperanza to give Phoebe the clearance so that she could be involved in rescuing their son.

Fourthly, Phoebe knew then that they couldn't go back to Iseul because the latter would tell Esperanza. If "Angel" used to work with Keenan, she might still have friends in Mendenhall Security, who could end up being moles, jeopardizing Jamie's rescue. Phoebe had to find other help.

"What did you do for Angel?" Joe's voice was harsh, but his Sig Sauer on Newell's temple was harsher. He pressed the nozzle hard until Newell gave up.

"Don't shoot. Please." The coward was covered with straw from the bed on the ground when he'd struggled with Joe just before being tasered.

"Then talk."

"She told me to take the kids to a meeting place in Gatlinburg, and I did." Newell wheezed. "I dropped them off, and that was the last time I saw them."

"Your own son too!" Phoebe yelled at him.

"He might not be mine."

"He's an innocent child."

"Twenty thousand dollars."

"You jerk!" And Phoebe almost whacked him with the spading fork, but Joe got to him first.

In the distance, sirens blared.

CHAPTER 5

His two-hour emergency meeting over, Keenan grabbed a to-go sandwich from the lodge restaurant to eat at his office desk.

He didn't expect to see Phoebe in the dining room. It was less than one hour to closing time. Yet, he took a quick look anyway, just in case.

Nope. She's not here.

Phoebe must've gone to the hospital to meet April and check on Mrs. Madison. It was a good thing for her to keep busy. Otherwise, she'd go crazy with Jamie gone and all.

Keenan plopped down in his office chair, and asked God to bless his food and find his son. He prayed that Phoebe wouldn't do anything he wouldn't.

He finished his sandwich, and then opened a secure window to speak with Esperanza in Atlanta. She was the only person on the screen until she pushed her laptop away on the conference table, allowing the video camera a wider angle.

Keenan spotted Marie sitting in the next chair over. She was eating a sandwich for dinner. She waved to the camera without a word.

"You're early." Esperanza was drinking an after-dinner smoothie.

Keenan glanced at his phone. "By thirty minutes."

Esperanza leaned forward in her chair. "How are you and Phoebe doing?"

"Waiting for Kyle to update us. They're searching everywhere."

"If this was an ordinary case, you and Phoebe would be out there organizing a community search for your own son, wouldn't you?"

Keenan nodded.

"But you're not," Esperanza added.

"Kyle can do more than we can."

"Wrong answer, Keenan." Esperanza leaned back. "You're not combing the neighborhood yourself not because you don't want to interfere with police work, but because you know Jamie is no longer in town."

"Gut instinct."

"And you also know who might have abducted him," Esperanza added.

"You do too." Keenan sighed.

"When are you going to tell your wife what you know?"

Keenan wasn't sure how to respond.

"If you're not transparent with her, you will wreck your marriage." Esperanza looked serious.

"But her clearance..."

"You know that I've already asked her to take over the deputy director job, and Joe is ready to train her, but she is still praying about it. The fact that I offered her the position meant that she's cleared the background check. Besides, she's been working for me for nine years, but you knew that."

"If I solve it, then things will get back to normal. What's there to explain then?" Keenan said.

"You mean you'd try to secretly solve it?"

"Yeah."

That way, he didn't have to explain his relationship with Noreen before she met her husband. It wasn't something Keenan was proud of, but he wanted to come clean with Phoebe in all areas of his life. He just didn't expect to have to do it this soon.

"You alone, the solver of all problems?" There was an edge to Esperanza's tone.

"Noreen is targeting me because we almost dated, remember? It seems that she can't see me being happy now when her own life is in shambles. In a way, it's my fault. I don't want anyone else to get hurt."

"It's not your fault that a former MI6 operative is deranged," Marie finally spoke.

Why would Noreen Nair—formerly known as Susan Atkins—put aside an illustrious career at the UK's Mission Intelligence, Section 6, and go rogue? Keenan knew the answer, of course.

"It's me she wants," Keenan admitted. "She thinks I ruined her marriage. Now she's getting back at me."

"Let me get this straight. You, the Lone Ranger, are going to singlehandedly solve Noreen's problems and rescue your son from her." There was a sharpness to Esperanza's voice that made Keenan question his own judgment.

"I know Noreen. I'll reason with her." It was all the defense Keenan had.

"Right, let's do just that. I'll give you a medal when you return from your conversation." Esperanza frowned.

"Okay."

"No, Keenan. I was being sarcastic." Esperanza slurped the rest of her smoothie through a fat straw. "Wake up, man. Noreen has a vendetta, but not against you alone. She hates me too. She and I were both in MI6, remember?"

She shook her head. "I'm still stunned that Noreen is alive. For so many years, we thought that she was dead."

"So dead, in fact, that her own Qatari husband has remarried," Marie added.

"With two kids." Esperanza checked her watch.

"Now we find out that Noreen is not only alive, but she has an axe to grind." Keenan steeled his resolve.

"She's coming after your son because she thinks that she can hurt you that way," Esperanza said. "Don't think for a moment that she will let your wife get a pass."

Keenan's hand trembled. It had never happened before.

"And when she has murdered your son, it will be too late for you to come clean to Phoebe. If she divorces you, it would be a light sentence for you."

Esperanza had a way with words sometimes. However, she always spoke the truth.

"Why not take this golden opportunity to

strengthen your relationship with your wife?" Esperanza asked.

"She's okay." *I think.*

"She looks okay, but she's not. You're distancing yourself from her because you're afraid that your secret will leak out."

"Secret?" Keenan was sure that he'd told Phoebe almost everything that he could tell her.

"Yes. The one you can't tell her about. That one."

Marie glanced at Esperanza sitting next to her, and then to the laptop. "What secret?"

"He knows what I'm talking about." Esperanza drew a deep breath.

Keenan truly didn't know what to do. "If I tell Phoebe everything, she might leave me."

"If you tell her nothing, she might also leave you." Esperanza's voice was stern. At this point, she was behaving more like an older sister or a young aunt than his employer. "Take your poison pill."

"What should I do?" Keenan thought aloud.

"You should trust God, not yourself or even Phoebe. Can the God who brought the two of you together in holy matrimony also keep your marriage intact?"

"Of course He can."

"Then what are you worried about?"

Esperanza's question resonated in Keenan's head. Even though he knew the truth, putting it into practice was harder. Then again, the Bible had spoken about doing the right thing.

Therefore, to him who knows to do good and does not do it, to him it is sin.

How could he refuse the truth in James 4:17?

Esperanza waved her hands in the air. "Keenan, you're officially off this operation."

"What?"

"In the grand scheme of things, your relationship with your wife is more important than whether you lead this operation or not," Esperanza added. "Put down your pride, old friend."

Pride? Did Keenan have pride? Why would Esperanza mention the word?

Esperanza knew her Bible, so Keenan was thankful that she didn't pull the Bible card on him. Even so, her mention of the word triggered his recollection of another verse in the same chapter he'd just recalled. James 4:6 spoke of pride as well.

> But He gives more grace. Therefore He says:
> "God resists the proud,
> But gives grace to the humble."

Did this mean that Keenan should humble himself and come clean to his wife about Noreen? He wouldn't have to do a thing if Noreen had stayed dead. However, she hadn't died, and therefore, her problems continued. If her problems, with all their tentacles, reached his family...

Well, they might already have arrived at his doorstep.

"As your old friend Lamar's trusted partner and the love of his life, as well as your current boss, I'm advising you to go home to your wife to provide her with some emotional support. Treasure her."

Treasure her.

Keenan was sure he did. Why wouldn't he treasure the woman whom God had brought his way to share his life with?

Then again, something inside Keenan felt strongly that he had to take down Noreen.

"Let me stay until we find Omar," Keenan said.

"No. Are you kidding me? Didn't you hear a thing I said?" Esperanza was rarely angry, but she was now.

"Please? Omar remarried and has two kids with his new wife," Keenan said. "Now the entire family has disappeared from the face of the earth. I think these two missing cases are related, and the dot connecting the two is Noreen."

"Thank you for your opinion. We can handle it."

"Do you want me to get on my robotic knees and beg?" Keenan asked. "I am quite confident that if we find Noreen, we find my son."

It was a flying leap from Maysie's ex-husband, and Keenan had no proof. However, once upon a time, during down time in a joint operation, he'd disclosed to Noreen that when he married someday, he'd want a son.

And he'd name him James.

James O'Tierney.

At that time, Noreen had thought that Keenan meant that he'd marry her. How she'd jumped to that conclusion was beyond him, but she had somehow done so.

Keenan felt guilty that he had shared too much of his own personal thoughts with her. She might have felt led on.

When Keenan rejected Noreen's invitations to

spend weekends alone with her, she was devastated. A few weeks later, she went on a mission in Qatar and married Omar Nair on a whim without as much as a background check on the man.

To this date, Keenan hadn't disclosed any of that to Phoebe.

"Aren't you going to start the meeting?" Keenan asked. "If you don't want me to stay in the operation, I can at least brief you all on what I've done thus far."

That should buy him time.

Before Esperanza could reply, her phone buzzed. "Hey Iseul, whassup?"

Iseul Kim worked at the Binary Systems headquarters in Atlanta. Whenever Cayson or Leland were unavailable, it was Iseul who answered the phone when Esperanza called for technical help.

"She what?" Esperanza almost yelled into the phone. "Hold on. Let me put you on speaker. Please repeat what you just told me."

Iseul's voice came through loud and clear. "Phoebe obtained the home surveillance videos from April and found something. Then she and Joe drove half an hour to an abandoned barn and made a citizen's arrest of a drunk Newell Greer and rescued an unconscious Maysie. Newell is in police custody, and Maysie is in the hospital."

Esperanza glanced at the camera. "While we're sitting here, chatting about the merits of transparency, your wife is out there kicking down doors."

"You should promote her right away," Marie said.

"I've tried, and I'm still trying."

Keenan ignored the two while he processed what

Iseul had just told them. "Keenan here, Iseul. Two questions for you, if I may?"

"Go ahead," Iseul said.

"First question. What did Phoebe see on the videos?"

"I saw the same videos and so did MMPD—who have their own copy that they'd obtained from April independently of Phoebe," Iseul said. "All it showed was Marcia letting Newell into the house. Maysie came downstairs and was frantic. Newell beat her up. At that point, Mrs. Madison shot him.

She missed the torso and only nicked his arm.

Although bleeding, Newell subdued her. A woman—probably his accomplice—entered the house and pointed a gun at Maysie's head. At that point, Mrs. Madison surrendered her weapon.

The two abductors then took all three adults and two boys out of the house and shoved them into their van without a license tag. There you have it in a nutshell."

"I want to see the video," Keenan said. He couldn't tell from this third-hand account what Phoebe actually saw that made her know where to find Newell.

"Do you have April Moreno's number?" Iseul asked.

"I do." Esperanza raised her hand. "I'll call her."

"What's your second question?" Iseul asked. "I have to go soon. Kelvin's out, and I'm filling in for him in the machine room."

"Again?" Esperanza asked.

"Yeah." Iseul said no more.

As far as Keenan knew, Kelvin Gallagher was the system administrator at Binary Systems. While the employees had different roles at the company, they were all hackers. Most of the time, they worked for government entities, but since the founders, Cayson Yang and his cousin Leland, knew Esperanza, they had made an exception for their entire company to help Mendenhall Security whenever needed.

"Second question. Do you know what Newell told Phoebe in the barn?" Keenan asked.

"Unfortunately, no. Sorry. She talked to the police. That's all I know."

Keenan knew he couldn't call Kyle, who wouldn't disclose their investigations to him. Keenan had to find out things on his own using Mendenhall Security's resources.

"I could pay Maysie a visit in the hospital," Keenan said.

"She was unconscious in the barn," Iseul reminded him.

"Yeah, but for how long?" Esperanza turned to the camera. "I think it's a good idea to talk to Maysie."

"Maybe Phoebe and I can go see her together." Keenan couldn't wait to be reunited with his wife. It was bad enough that he had kept secrets from her, but now he wanted to be on the same page with her.

When he saw her next, he'd disclose everything to her.

Keenan reached for his phone. Phoebe's locator app had been turned off, but two hours ago, she—or at least her phone—was at Joe Brannigan's house.

He checked his home security system. Phoebe

hadn't been home since they'd both left the house together.

He called Phoebe.

No answer.

In fact, her voicemail kicked in right away. Had she shut off her phone?

He called Joe Brannigan. Also no answer.

Where are you, Phoebe?

Panic set in.

"Espy, could you try to call Phoebe?" Keenan realized his voice was slightly on edge.

Esperanza tried. "She's not answering."

"She handed Newell to the police and then disappeared." Keenan guessed what might have happened. "What did Newell tell Phoebe at the barn?"

"Iseul, could you find Phoebe?" Esperanza asked.

"I can try."

"Please and thank you." Keenan regretted not staying with Phoebe after dinner. He had let her drive off alone while he attended a meeting—or tried to—that mattered little in the grand scheme of things.

Phoebe was out there fighting hard to find their son while he sat here conjecturing that Noreen had taken his son. He didn't want Phoebe to know about Noreen.

How foolish am I? Forgive me, Lord.

"I've got to go find my wife." Keenan sprung up from his chair.

"Calm down," Esperanza said. "Let Iseul do some tracking first."

"Phoebe could be in danger."

"Don't underestimate your wife." Esperanza

motioned for him to sit down. "There's no need for knee-jerk reactions."

Keenan sat back down. "I was going to drive over to Joe's house to talk to him. He was the other person in the barn. He might know something."

"Your chief of police already talked to Phoebe and Joe, but we have no access to the MMPD system—at least not legally," Iseul said. "However, we can always try to track down Joe and Phoebe."

"Please do that." Keenan realized how different Iseul was compared to Leland and Cayson. The latter two were proactive. Iseul seemed to be a regular employee, taking orders, but not making big independent decisions.

Different roles for different people.

"How soon can you track down Joe?" Keenan asked.

"I think twenty minutes," Iseul said.

"Phoebe?"

"Longer. I don't have enough data from her to feed into my AI tracker."

"Then start with the easy one: Joe," Esperanza said.

Keenan picked up his phone. "I'm going to drive over to his house. That was Phoebe's last known location. It'll take fifteen minutes for me to get there. If he's there, I'll talk to him. If he's not there, I'll call Iseul."

"Go, Keenan." Esperanza nodded. "Go find your wife and kid."

At that moment, a sense of desperation overcame Keenan. By attending this meeting that hadn't started, he felt that he had abandoned Phoebe to her own devises.

He was grateful that Joe was there for Phoebe, but Keenan should've been her support system for such a time as this.

Still, no matter how bad he felt, he had to press on.

CHAPTER 6

K eenan is not telling me something.

The thought continued to bother Phoebe on the flight in the turboprop cargo plane from Gatlinburg-Pigeon Forge Airport in Sevierville, Tennessee, to the Gwinnett County Airport – Briscoe Field in Lawrenceville, Georgia.

It was clear to Phoebe that Keenan had known the mastermind behind their son's abduction. Instead of sharing the information with her, he'd gone to a virtual meeting with Esperanza.

She didn't like his modus operandi. Not one bit.

This wasn't the time to play hide-and-seek with Phoebe. No, she wasn't saying that her husband was weak, but that he needed to do some course correction to right their marriage. If he kept hiding secrets from her—like his past work that could affect Phoebe and Jamie—then their trust in each other would continue to erode.

Every minute that they didn't find Jamie was another minute that he was closer to a point of no return. Child trafficking was no joke. Not that

Keenan had taken it lightly, but why couldn't he see that Phoebe could help?

That was to say, instead of both of them working separately, wouldn't it be better if they had worked together as a team instead?

If it had come down to security clearance, Phoebe was about to accept the deputy director position at Mendenhall Retreat. Wasn't that enough to put her on the same level as Keenan?

From her jump seat, Phoebe glanced to her right, but there was no window to look out of. She was strapped to one of two seats facing boxes of cargo tied down in front of her in the cabin. Beside her, Joe Brannigan was taking a nap and snoring.

They were both wearing aviation headsets so that Jessica in the cockpit could communicate with them. This was the only intercom in the small cargo plane.

At first, Phoebe wanted to take a commercial flight to Atlanta, but it meant having to drive more than an hour to Knoxville. Then Joe called his daughter, Jessica, a pilot who owned her own cargo business. She had been a commercial airline pilot until she retired and moved to Gatlinburg to be closer to her aging father after his wife passed away. She still had a house in Atlanta, which she would stay in whenever she was in town.

Jessica wasn't supposed to fly out to Miami until the next morning, but she decided to leave tonight on account of her dad's great adventure. Phoebe could tell that Jessica was worried about her father, but Phoebe promised to take good care of Joe.

Phoebe was happy to see such a good relationship between Joe and his daughter. She reflected on her own rapport with her dad, who had changed his flight so that he could meet her in Atlanta with a suitcase of cash for their mission.

However, she was disappointed in her husband. She wanted to cry because Keenan hadn't trusted her with information that she had to find out herself independent of him or Esperanza. Well, to be fair, she had help from Joe Brannigan, who still held the deputy director position at Mendenhall Retreat.

Phoebe closed her eyes and recalled the events that had happened since she left dinner at the Mendenhall Lodge. She flinched when her memory arrived at the incident in the barn.

Joe stirred in the other jump seat. He yawned and turned his head toward Phoebe. "You okay?"

Phoebe nodded.

He patted his own shoulder. "Cry on here."

"No need. I'm a big girl." Phoebe dried her eyes.

"You're very brave. Also, I'm glad you paid attention in Espy's Krav Maga class and in all the training she has given you. Without you, I wouldn't have been able to take down Newell."

Joe smiled. Wrinkles on his face reminded Phoebe of Dad's face. Then Phoebe felt bad that Dad was meeting them in Atlanta because Dad was not prepared for what they were about to do. Fortunately, Dad was bringing Garrett with him.

"We made the right move not to go back to Iseul after we talked to Newell," Joe said.

Talked to Newell?

Joe had tried to beat the tar out of him.

"Good thing you know someone else," Phoebe said.

Joe shrugged. "Dmitri and I are friends."

He had used his connection to Dmitri Proskouri-akoff—whose background Phoebe wasn't supposed to ask about—to access the services of a couple of young hackers who hacked into Newell's phone to find out who had picked up the two boys in Gatlinburg.

College kids Havilah and Asher, the two nine-teen-year-olds at Still Salvage in the Still Waters community near Dmitri's farmhouse in North Georgia, hadn't done this kind of work before, but they aced it on the first try—no doubt with Dmitri's vast network.

The duo traced the abductors from Gatlinburg, where Newell had last seen them, all the way to Peachtree City. That might have been the drop-off point.

Phoebe told herself to be patient, but she couldn't make her heartbeat slow down.

How much patience would it require to wait for the safe return of her son? From the surveillance time-stamped, it had only been about six hours since Jamie had been abducted.

She placed both palms on her chest, trying to calm herself. She realized then that the patience she could conjure up by the sheer power of her will would be inadequate. And yet, she didn't want the patience of Job. That biblical character had lost all of his adult children.

Please, Lord, let Jamie live.

She tried to recall all the Bible passages she had read that might apply to this. Her mind drew a blank.

I am too stressed out to even think.

She drew a deep breath. She reached into her

pockets to find her phone so that she could look up some Bible verses—

No phone.

She realized how dependent she was on her phone, and how distracted she had been, leaving it on Joe's kitchen counter.

Once again, she'd have to borrow Joe's phone, but not right now. He was fast asleep.

Quietly, Phoebe thanked God for Joe, his vast resources and surprising connections, including Dmitri and the hackers from Still Salvage. She wondered if Dmitri was training Havilah and Asher, just as he had trained Leland Yang-Joule years ago.

"Thank You, Jesus, for those two kids," she whispered.

Havilah and Asher had been the ones who'd traced Newell's phone call to an Atlanta number, and then extrapolated the precise location of where the kids might be auctioned off in the metropolitan area.

Unfortunately, that was all they had. They had no idea where the kids were kept until they were sold.

It was enough.

According to Dmitri, the auction venue moved. The human traders were always on high alert regarding police activities in the area. Right now, the auction had been scheduled to take place in a warehouse in Peachtree City, but it could move at the last minute.

If they moved, then Phoebe and her ragtag team would have to chase after them. How long would it go on? Until Jamie came home.

Patience.

Phoebe expelled a breath. "Lord, please give me patience."

"Patience?" Joe rubbed his eyes. It looked like he'd dozed off once more.

"I'm sorry. Did I speak too loudly?" Phoebe asked.

"I wasn't sleeping properly anyway," Joe said. "Sounds like you need patience in a hurry, like instantly, like right now."

"Are you making fun of me?" Phoebe wrinkled her nose.

"No, no." Joe swiped his phone and searched his Bible app. "I just want to share one of my favorite trench verses."

"Trench verses?"

"Verses you need when stuck in a trench with enemy fire all above you."

"Oh? Like in World War I?" *How old are you, Joe?*

"It's a word picture, child." Joe smiled. "James 1:2-4. Ready to hear it?"

"Yes, sir."

"I'm going to read this verse aloud. Your job is to look for the milestone sequence. Got it?"

Phoebe nodded and listened attentively as Joe recited the Bible passage from James 1:2-4.

My brethren, count it all joy when you fall into various trials, knowing that the testing of your faith produces patience. But let patience have its perfect work, that you may be perfect and complete, lacking nothing.

"What sequence do you see?" Joe asked.

"Before we get to the steps, there is the attitude," Phoebe said. "James 1:2 says that I have to approach this world of trouble with an attitude of joy. Not that I'm delighted to be in trouble, precisely, but that the joy of the Lord is my strength through these trials."

"Good. I like that reminder from Nehemiah 8:10b also." And Joe proceeded to recite that verse.

Do not sorrow, for the joy of the Lord is your strength.

"Therefore, cloaked with the joy of the Lord, you can now tell me the points that we need to bear in mind from James 1:2-4 as we fly out to Atlanta to rescue your son." Joe put away his phone, perhaps so that he didn't leave it out and forget about it.

If Phoebe had done that back at Joe's house, she would still have her phone with her. However, she'd been absentminded, with her brain preoccupied with finding Jamie.

Now God was reminding her through Joe that she needed to essentially calm down and claim Bible verses that God had already written for her by way of James.

"James 1:3 reminds me that when I 'fall into various trials,' I need to know that my faith is being tested," Phoebe said. "This testing of my faith can produce patience in me or pulverize me altogether. Therefore, James 1:4 warns me to let God work out the patience in me so that I will emerge from this 'complete, lacking nothing.' That is to say, God is with me to test me, try me, train me."

Joe nodded. "Me too. I'm being tested as well."

"Then with God's help, let's emerge victorious in Christ." Phoebe made the victory sign with her fingers.

And they burst into an a cappella duet of the old hymn, "Victory in Jesus." Neither of them could remember all the lyrics written by Eugene M. Bartlett, but both sang the chorus with gusto repeatedly, with Joe slightly tone-deaf.

Halfway through, Jessica joined in from the cockpit. Her soprano blended well with Phoebe's mezzo, with Joe's tenor.

"All right, people," Jessica cut them off when they had sung the chorus ad infinitum. "We're landing in about twenty-five minutes."

"I'll make sure to put my seat upright and my seat tray up." Joe made a motion at an imaginary tray in front of him.

It made Phoebe laugh.

"Feeling better now?" Joe nudged her with his elbow.

Phoebe nodded. "Nothing like a Bible verse and a good dose of a church hymn. Thank you, Joe."

"To God be the glory." He folded his arms over his chest and closed his eyes. "Now be quiet while I take a ten-minute power nap."

Phoebe chuckled. She closed her eyes and rehearsed her plan.

Once Jessica's plane landed at Briscoe field, it would take another hour and a half for Phoebe and Joe to drive to Peachtree City on the other side of Atlanta. Halfway there, they'd stop at the Hartsfield-Jackson Atlanta International Airport to pick up Dad and Garrett, who would have arrived on their flight from Savannah.

Four people with no backups were about to enter the pit to rescue two boys from human traffickers. Even if Jessica had come with them, her background as a former commercial airplane pilot wouldn't help one bit.

Are we fools?

Phoebe wished that Keenan were here. He had the experience and the know-how. If "Angel" was his enemy, then he surely knew how to deal with her.

Oblivious to her thoughts, Joe seemed to take it all in stride, as though this was his last battle before final retirement.

Or death.

"Want something to drink?" Joe spoke into the headset's microphone.

All three of them heard it.

"There's bottled water and soda in the cooler in here." Jessica's voice came through Phoebe's headset.

"I'll just have water," Phoebe replied. "Thank you."

Joe unbuckled and shuffled away. He favored his right leg, and Phoebe felt sorry that she had put so much strain on him by letting him accompany her to the barn.

Then again, Joe had insisted on going—and doing it before they called the police.

In retrospect, it had been the most foolish move that Phoebe had ever done in her professional life. She knew she'd hear an earful from Keenan and Esperanza later, but for now, their trip to the barn had been a success.

Jessica's cargo plane landed at Briscoe Field at ten o'clock at night. They didn't have to rent a vehicle because Jessica would let them use her car, which she had parked at the small regional airport. That way, she didn't have to rent a car whenever she came to Atlanta.

Jessica didn't have to fly to Miami until morning, and wanted badly to tag along, but Joe told her no. They argued, but Joe won. So the plan remained the same as Joe had set it up: Jessica would give them a ride to Atlanta, and then go on her merry way. Joe and Phoebe alone would go to Peachtree City.

Phoebe suspected that Jessica was worried about her dad. Even though orphaned Jessica had been thirteen years old when Joe and his wife adopted her, she had grown close to the couple, both sixty-nine years old when the adoption papers had been signed. For the next nineteen years, Jessica had been a blessing to the family. Thirty-two years old now, her only regret was not working closer to home, especially when her adopted mother had been ill.

Jessica's life was similar to Phoebe's, although it also differed. Adopted as well, Phoebe's life had taken a turn when she ran away from her adopted family in Savannah. She was lost as a teenager and ended up wandering around in Tennessee, doing odd jobs in tourist towns. One day, Phoebe worked late at night and ended up getting physically assaulted.

She wandered into Mountain Chapel in Sevierville and found help. A couple of months later, she discovered that she was pregnant. She decided to keep the baby since the baby was an innocent individual.

The Mountain Chapel pastor and his wife turned out to be childless. They had prayed for many years for a child. As an answer to prayer, they decided to adopt Phoebe's daughter and named her Alexi.

The pastor's wife, Darlene, kept Phoebe updated on Alexi's growth, and during one of their many phone calls, Darlene witnessed to Phoebe and told her about Jesus Christ.

Phoebe appreciated that someone had prayed for her. Still going from job to job, she eventually ended up working at the Misty Mountain Funeral Home in Misty Mountain, where Mrs. Madison had invited her to a Bible study. There, Phoebe finally met the Lord.

She completed her GED and found a second job at the Mendenhall Retreat front desk. There, Esperanza took Phoebe under her wing.

When Alexi was seven years old, Phoebe met Keenan, and her life changed. They had been together for seven years, married for six, and had a son, now four years old.

Perhaps it was time for Phoebe to make the first move and call Keenan. She couldn't expect Keenan to divulge any secrets that Mendenhall Security might not allow him to. Doing so might put his entire team at risk, especially the people who had anything to do with "Angel."

However, skirting around him—with Joe in tow—might be a terrible move.

Phoebe felt bad that her team had involved not only Joe, but her own father, a former riverboat operator who had never used a handgun—except for that one time he went hunting for wild boars in Florida, even though he'd ended up using a bow and arrow instead.

Garrett was fine because he was an active duty Green Beret. However, he'd be the only one who might have to protect them all. Joe could brandish a weapon, but his bad knee might be his Achilles heel.

Oh, what have I done?

It felt like Phoebe was about to bring a bigger disaster into these people's lives. She wondered how her boss—that fearless Esperanza Diaz-Mendenhall— felt whenever she had to send people into harm's way.

Was it too late to backtrack?

"Landing in five minutes," Jessica said through the headset. "Dad, please return to your seat and buckle up."

"Okay, okay." Joe sounded frustrated. "I was looking for the bathroom."

"There's no lavatory onboard, Dad. This is a small cargo plane. Every available space is for cargo."

"I'm sure there's a bathroom at the airport," Phoebe suggested.

"Yes. Can you hold it for five minutes, Dad?" Jessica asked.

"I guess so." Joe returned to his jump seat without any bottled water that he was supposed to bring Phoebe.

Phoebe didn't bring it up. She wasn't that thirsty.

The cargo plane touched down on the single runway, and Jessica slowed down the plane during the rollout. As the plane taxied, Jessica kept Phoebe and Joe informed because neither of them could look outside to see what was happening.

Phoebe closed her eyes and prayed silently.

Lord, I don't know what I am getting into. All the training I've received at Mendenhall seems inadequate. I've never left the training center, so to speak. Never been in the field. Already, Joe and I have tied up Newell and threatened him. I think we could be in some sort of trouble with the law, even though Joe said that we were making a citizen's arrest. Besides, Joe made sure that I wasn't the one who beat him up.

Phoebe drew a deep breath.

And then there's all that hacking that Still Salvage is still doing for us. It seems that if we asked Binary Systems, we would get away with gray areas. But those college kids at Still Salvage might be in trouble for helping us—even though Joe has the clearance and authority. Then again, he called Dmitri, who has ties to Russia. What a mess!

As the plane made its way to its designated parking stand near the cargo warehouse, Phoebe was fully aware that she was getting closer to rescuing her son or closer to death. Either way, she was no longer in her safe house on top of the Great Smoky Mountains.

Phoebe clasped her hands together to prevent them from shaking.

Lord, please save Jamie. If I end up in jail because we have no idea which things we did broke the law or not, then I'll go to jail. As long as Jamie is safe and sound. Please, Lord, rescue my son. Bring him home in one piece, and help him to recover from his trauma. Let him go on to lead a full and fruitful life. Don't let him forget to visit me in prison.

The aircraft finally stopped moving, and Jessica shut down the engine.

"Is it time to disembark?" Joe asked.

"Yes, sir," Jessica said. "I'll come get you in a second."

"No need. We can walk to the door ourselves." Joe chuckled.

Phoebe unbuckled her seat belt. Her legs wobbled when she tried to get up. A strong arm gripped her as her entire weight leaned on it.

She looked up.

Keenan's eyes bored into hers. He frowned.

Phoebe burst into tears.

CHAPTER 7

"After eight years of training you, it would be a waste of all my time, effort, and resources not to let you have first dibs at the deputy director position at the retreat." Esperanza sat in the same row as Phoebe in the eight-seater SUV.

Phoebe nodded. She had wanted to take the job, but she hadn't had the time to tell Esperanza yet. It seemed that Keenan hadn't said anything to the Mendenhall Retreat owner yet. So poor Esperanza was now still trying to sell the position to Phoebe.

"Joe said that you've exceeded your job description as the office manager. You've been invaluable to him, filling in for him when he's unwell," Esperanza continued. "He wants to retire after his knee replacement next month."

Then Esperanza waited for Phoebe to say something.

Phoebe was still taking in and rehashing all that had happened when their cargo plane landed at Briscoe Field, only to be greeted by Keenan and Esperanza at the airport. They had flown out of

Gatlinburg as soon as they'd figured out where Phoebe had gone. Their state-of-the-art private plane had been faster, and they had arrived ten minutes before Jessica landed her turboprop.

Ushered into an SUV parked outside the cargo warehouse, they took off for Peachtree City some forty minutes away.

Slowly, Phoebe realized that Esperanza knew everything.

"You were two steps ahead of us though," Esperanza said to Phoebe.

"Of course," Joe replied on her behalf. His voice came from the row behind Phoebe.

In that row of bucket seats, Joe and Keenan were poring over a laptop. Phoebe heard Joe tell Keenan about what Havilah and Asher had done for them. Keenan said something about letting those two people brief Iseul at Binary Systems so that they could all be on the same page.

In the last row, the backseat against the back windows of the SUV, a silent Garrett looked out of the side window. Next to him, Dad had fallen asleep, held up by his safety belt.

In the front two seats were Esperanza's people. One was driving, and the other was navigating.

Missing from the SUV was Jessica Brannigan, Joe's daughter. She had to fly her cargo to Miami in the morning, and didn't have time to tag along on their mission.

The company-owned SUV was heading south on Interstate 85 toward Peachtree City, where the auction house had been located by none other than Havilah and Asher.

No doubt Esperanza might seek to recruit them, but Still Salvage probably wouldn't let them go.

"Tell her yes." Joe prodded Phoebe's shoulder from behind her.

When Phoebe glanced at him, she saw Keenan's stare, as though he was saying, "Don't touch my wife!"

That seemed to be Keenan's first outburst of the night. He hadn't been mad or upset at Phoebe for flying to Atlanta without him. He was slightly irritated that Phoebe's stepbrother was present, but they had a good relationship with each other, so it was almost like a reunion between two old friends.

Keenan needn't have worried. The last thing Garrett would do was to try to impress anyone. He was low key and a man of few words. In fact, he hadn't spoken at all on the drive to Peachtree City.

It wasn't that he didn't want to be there. Phoebe knew his personality well enough to say that Garrett was worried about his step-nephew. He had last seen Jamie at Thanksgiving in Savannah when Jamie was three years old. Jamie liked Uncle Garrett more than Isaac, his other uncle. Jamie would hold Garrett's hand whenever they went out to eat, and chattered the most when Uncle Garrett was in the room.

"Tell her yes, Phoebe," Joe repeated. This time he didn't touch Phoebe.

"I wanted to call HR this afternoon as soon as Jamie went missing, actually. However, I wanted to pray about it some more," Phoebe said to Esperanza. "I didn't want to make an emotional decision because I knew that the only reason I'd want the job right now was to get top secret clearance with you so that I could go out there to rescue my son. After I calmed down, I remembered that Joe already had access. If I could get him to help me, I wouldn't need the deputy director position."

"Meaning what? You don't want the job?" Esperanza looked hurt.

"I do want the job, but I don't know if this is the right time."

"If you take the job, rescuing your son would be your first assignment."

"Oh?" Phoebe glanced behind her seat at Keenan.

To his credit, he said, "Darling, I'll support you whatever you decide to do with your career. After all, you've prayed about it. I'm with you."

He stopped right there.

"As long as?" Phoebe asked. She knew him well.

"If we can work together on the same team, all the better."

Same team?

What did he mean? They had already worked together at Mendenhall Retreat, but they were not technically in the same branch. While Phoebe was the office manager at Mendenhall Retreat, Keenan was a special operative at Mendenhall Security. While they lived together, Keenan was gone two thirds of the year on various assignments.

After a while, Keenan got tired of all that traveling.

How could Phoebe and Keenan be on the same team? Even with the new position, Phoebe would still be working at the retreat while Keenan would still be flying around all over the world with Esperanza.

"We can put you on the same team," Esperanza said. "Just so happens that I've been thinking of creating a security team to protect the residents of Mendenhall Retreat. That way, we're not redirecting resources from Mendenhall Security whenever something happens at the retreat."

"What do you mean?" Keenan asked. "Are you moving MS out of MR?"

"You can look at it that way. I'm trying to spend more time in Atlanta. I'll still go to the retreat a few times a year—say, for quarterly meetings—but I can't expect the retreat deputy director to also be the chief of security."

"So are you making executive decisions as we're driving around?" Joe asked.

"Isn't it good that I own it all?" Esperanza laughed. "Although I miss Lamar terribly. If he were here, I wouldn't have to worry about these things."

Absentmindedly, Esperanza touched her diamond necklace that Lamar had gifted her one year before he passed away. Esperanza had held that necklace and cried in front of Phoebe the first few years after Lamar's death. Eventually, as time wore on, Esperanza cried less and less, though she still always touched the necklace at his memory.

Phoebe wasn't sure how else to help the forty-something widow but simply listened to her and kept her company whenever she wanted to talk or reminisce about her good old days.

Phoebe felt bad for Esperanza. It must have been a horrible thing to lose a spouse whom she loved and who'd loved her back. Their married life had been cut short by one senseless act.

No doubt, Esperanza would someday hunt down that murderer.

Meanwhile, she had accepted that Lamar was gone, and she had to move on in her own life.

"How can we help?" Phoebe asked.

"Good response." Esperanza smiled. "I need you to be my deputy director in charge of the entire Mendenhall Retreat. You can give me the answer now or later."

What would stop Phoebe? Whether today or the following week, wouldn't her answer be the same?

Alternatively, if she said no, Esperanza might find a better person to take the job.

Well, in that case, the position might not be for her, right?

Esperanza turned to Keenan. "I'm thinking of appointing you as the chief of security at the retreat. It's a new position. You'd have to staff it, but you can't take my people from Mendenhall Security. You won't need to travel much anymore, and you can work with your wife in the same building all year round."

"Wow. That's an answer to our prayer for more family time." Keenan looked at Phoebe.

She nodded in agreement. "Then I'll take the deputy director job."

Esperanza nearly leapt out of her seat. However, the safety belt held her in place. "I knew that'd do the trick."

"That means you're going to be short one person at Mendenhall Security," Phoebe reminded Esperanza.

"I'm always hiring." Esperanza glanced over at Garrett.

Uh-oh.

Phoebe nearly laughed.

Garrett wrinkled his eyebrows. "Me?"

"Yeah, you." Phoebe pointed. "How many years do you have left in the Army?"

"I have one more year, and then I'll transition to the Reserves," Garrett replied.

"As an Army Reserve Green Beret?" Phoebe asked.

Garrett nodded.

"Do you plan on working full time during the week in some sort of civilian job?" Esperanza asked.

"I haven't thought that far." It was all Garrett needed to say to make Esperanza stop asking.

Still, Phoebe was certain that now that Garrett was on Esperanza's radar, she would not let up.

Outside the SUV, night rain began to fall again.

They had left Interstate 85 before Phoebe realized it. The SUV was now on Senoia Road, which changed its name to Joel Cowan Parkway.

"You knew how to get this far, didn't you?" Esperanza asked.

"Yes, ma'am," Phoebe said. "We knew the auction house was in Peachtree City, but we didn't know which building. So we figured we'd just get here and then find our way around. Right, Joe?"

"Right." Joe sounded upbeat even though it was past his bedtime.

"Iseul and Cayson just found it," Keenan announced.

Esperanza turned to Keenan. "Cayson is there too?"

"Yep," Keenan said. "Havilah and Asher updated Iseul, and she called Cayson for help. Cayson is with her now at the office. Leland is out of town."

With Cayson Yang in the machine room, they would have faster information at their fingertips. Phoebe had called him before in times past on behalf of Esperanza. The hacker was solid.

God had provided all the help they needed.

"Are Havilah and Asher continuing to help?" Phoebe asked.

"Observing," Esperanza corrected her.

"Good enough. They've been great, taking us this far."

"I know. I think talents need to be nurtured."

"That's why we all like you, Espy." Phoebe meant it.

It was closer to eleven o'clock now. Rain continued to fall as the SUV turned into an empty street. The street lights seemed to be out of order. The SUV pulled into what looked like a rundown office complex. The entire ground floor was for parking.

A garage door opened, and the SUV entered the garage. Next to their SUV was a utility van.

Once the garage door closed behind them, they all filed out of the SUV. They were greeted by a man and a woman whom Phoebe didn't recognize.

"Everything ready?" Esperanza asked.

The woman nodded. "The auction house doesn't allow weapons of any kind."

"Bummer." Esperanza followed her through a door into what looked like an old office. It was empty save for some old broken chairs and tables. Dust was everywhere.

Phoebe began to cough.

Keenan came over to see how she was doing.

"Dusty, is all." *Cough. Cough.*

Keenan produced a disposable mask out of his pocket. It was crumpled, but Phoebe took it out of the plastic bag and put it over her nose and mouth.

Once everyone had filed in, someone closed the door.

"Keenan, put Iseul and Cayson on speaker," Esperanza said.

"Yes, ma'am." Keenan set up his laptop on top of a dusty table. He turned up the volume.

In an encrypted window, Cayson's face appeared. He hadn't shaved, but the stubble could hardly be considered a beard. Maybe he was trying to grow one, but it wasn't working too well.

"Hey, Espy. Whassup?" Cayson asked.

"Terrible things of awful proportions. What's new?" Esperanza chuckled, then turned serious. "This time two four-year-old boys are in danger. Thank you for your help."

"Any time. Speed is the key in this matter," Cayson said. "So far, we know that 'Angel' is Noreen. No last name."

"Her real name is Susan Atkins," Esperanza said. "She used to work with us, back when my husband was still alive, and Mendenhall Security wasn't formed."

Even though Esperanza sounded serious and unemotional, Phoebe knew that every now and then she'd cry when she missed Lamar. Married without kids, they had been thinking of adopting. Unfortunately, he was murdered before they could expand their family.

Esperanza had immersed herself into work the

last seven years. She hadn't dated, hadn't remarried, and still kept everything as Lamar had arranged things in their log cabin behind the Mendenhall Lodge.

However, lately, she had increasingly been absent from Mendenhall Retreat because she had opened a Mendenhall Security branch office in Atlanta to be closer to VenomLabs, her biggest client. Word was that a merger with Dmitri's security firm was coming, but only Esperanza knew when that might happen.

Keenan looked at Phoebe. "Noreen blames me for her separation from her husband. Then she faked her own death and vanished for years. Nobody knew where she went."

He sounded professional, and Phoebe wondered what kind of secrets he wasn't telling her or anyone else. Her mind tried to splice what Keenan just said with the text message between Noreen and Newell.

He made my husband leave me. So now I make his son leave him.

Phoebe was apt to believe her own husband over Noreen. Perhaps Noreen was delusional when she messaged Newell. Perhaps it had been a ploy to gain Newell's sympathy.

Then again, why had Noreen purposefully skipped over Phoebe in her game of vengeance? Newell had been right that it would've been more logical had Noreen harmed Phoebe instead of a four-year-old kid.

Did Noreen know something that Phoebe didn't know?

Did Keenan know what Noreen knew?

"Meanwhile, after receiving her death certificate, Noreen's husband remarried," Esperanza said.

"A fake death certificate," Keenan added for good measure.

"In any case, Omar now lives in Spain with his new wife, and they have two kids." Esperanza looked around the room. "Are we all caught up?"

Phoebe felt that there wasn't enough to paint a picture, but she didn't care. "My purpose for coming to Atlanta is to rescue Jamie. For all we know, he might not be at the auction house tonight—although I'd believe what Havilah and Asher found."

"I can speak to that," Cayson said via the laptop video. "Iseul and I just confirmed that, yes, Jamie and Hanley have been taken to Peachtree City and, yes, they are on the auction block tonight at two o'clock. There are many people for sale, so in order to find these kids, we have to get inside the building."

"Espy and Keenan can't go," Phoebe said. "Noreen might have people on the ground."

"I agree," Joe said. "She could be watching the event live from overseas."

"I have to go in," Keenan said. "I'll wear a mask or something."

"No. If Jamie is there, we have only one chance to get him out." Esperanza pointed to Joe. "How are your legs?"

"I can't run, if that's what you're asking." Joe pointed to his knees. "Even after surgery next month, I may never be able to run again."

"You and Jerome stay here and work with Cayson and Iseul," Esperanza said to Joe.

Dad looked relieved that Esperanza hadn't

assigned him anything more than hanging out with Joe. This office space looked safe. As long as there was food and water, Dad was good to go. He could sleep on the floor if he had to.

"Let me go," Keenan pleaded.

Phoebe had never seen him beg. She didn't like it one bit. "How about you and Espy stay in the van? Garrett and I will go in as buyers. When we need help, we'll holler into our walkie talkie."

"You can't go either," Esperanza said to Phoebe.

"Why not?"

"I suspect that Noreen knows what you look like. Just because she skipped over you doesn't mean that she's ignoring you. It's entirely possible that she wants to get rid of Jamie first, and then she'll come after you."

"She wants to make me pay," Keenan said.

Esperanza waved to the man and woman who had met them in the garage. "Gita and Bryce will go in as buyers. They're driving a Bentley in the garage next door. Garrett, if you want, you can go in as a bodyguard for these buyers."

Phoebe knew that Esperanza was testing Garrett. As a member of the U.S. Army Special Forces, Garrett had already been trained. Going into the auction house was akin to going into a hostile territory. He could consider this a hostage rescue, which would have been covered in his counterterrorism training.

"Why are you sending Garrett when he's not on the payroll?" Keenan asked.

Jealous much?

"Contract work. How much do you charge per hour?" Esperanza asked Garrett.

He shrugged. "I don't know. Never done this before outside of my regular job."

"A thousand dollars an hour enough?"

Phoebe nearly laughed at the carrot Esperanza had dangled before Garrett.

"You paying for insurance?" Garrett asked.

"You're serious." Phoebe looked at her stepbrother.

"I've come this far. Anything to help little Jamie come home, Sis."

Phoebe's eyes stung.

"I'll be the representative from the family," Garrett said. "My job is so secretive that there's no photo of my bare face anywhere that Noreen could've unearthed."

Esperanza nodded. She waved to Gita. "Bring me a consultant contract." She paused. "Actually, make that three contracts. Even though Phoebe works for the retreat, this work falls under Mendenhall Security."

Dad pointed to himself. "Jerome Pendergast. A token civilian at your service. Give me something to do so I'm not worried sick about my grandson."

"How many people can the van in the garage carry?" Joe asked.

"We could all probably fit." Esperanza eyed Joe.

"If you let Jerome sign a contract, I think he can sit with me in the van. I'll be the bridge between us and Cayson and Iseul. That will free you up to plot and plan."

Phoebe signed the contract on Gita's tablet while

waiting to see if Esperanza was flexible enough to consider new suggestions after she had made a decision.

"We'll all be sitting with you and Keenan anyway," Joe added. "Consider this my last mission before retirement."

Esperanza was visibly moved.

"Okay." Her voice was raspy.

Maybe Joe reminded Esperanza of her deceased father. Maybe not. Phoebe had no idea. However, she had changed her mind because Joe had asked nicely. Sometimes it worked, but sometimes it didn't.

"We only have six armored catsuits and six pairs of smart glasses," Esperanza added. "So Joe and Jerome must absolutely stay in the van. It's your only armor."

"Yes, ma'am." Joe saluted her.

"What armored catsuits?" Phoebe asked just as the answer presented itself.

Even though she had been the office manager at Mendenhall Retreat, she had never heard of this catsuit, and Keenan had never mentioned it.

"It's a new thing that Mendenhall Security is testing for VenomLabs, along with everything else experimental, such as my prosthetics," Keenan said.

"The smart glasses too?" Phoebe asked.

"Well, those are made by VenomLabs, but they were made for Binary Systems specifically. So that's who we report back to if we find defects."

Within minutes, Keenan had ushered her into a closed office space to change into their armored catsuits.

"I haven't had a chance to talk to you since dinner," Keenan said.

"A lot has happened."

He lifted her hands and inspected the back of them and the palms. "Are you injured in any way?"

Phoebe shook her head. "Joe kept me safe."

"Should I thank him? Or should I thank God?"

"God sent Joe."

"It should've been me in the barn with you. Why leave me out?" Keenan kept his voice low.

Phoebe could sense an emotional undertow beneath that calm voice of his.

"When I found out that 'Angel' a.k.a. Noreen had connections to Mendenhall Security, I was..." Phoebe wasn't sure how to describe her emotions.

"Worried?"

"No. I was upset, Keenan. You could've told me about your history with Noreen."

"I'm sorry. Company secrets."

"If I'd known, I wouldn't have gone to Gatlinburg with Joe."

"But if you hadn't, you wouldn't have access to Newell's phone with the text messages on it." Keenan's voice softened. "And without the traces that Havilah and Asher had done, we wouldn't have found a direct link between the criminals whom Newell handed our son to and the auction house in Peachtree City."

"Wouldn't you and Espy have found the same information?"

"We might not have because Newell wouldn't speak to us. He knew about you because you've been a friend of the Madisons for years. You even attended Maysie's wedding, didn't you?"

"Yes, eight years ago."

"So there's a connection there that put Newell at ease."

Phoebe grabbed Keenan's wrist and pointed to his watch. "We better change."

"Okay."

Phoebe started to unbutton her blouse.

"Uh..." Keenan picked up his armored catsuit. "Why don't you change first, and I'll come back later."

"We're married. Are you shy?"

"I want to look at my wife."

"Dear husband, we have to go rescue our son from human traffickers. There is no time for dilly dallying."

"Yes, dear wife."

"How about you turn to face the other way and we change quickly?"

"I guess..."

"Just be disciplined enough not to turn around if that helps with your self control."

Keenan turned around and faced away from Phoebe. He continued talking. "At this rate, I'm surprised that we only have one child."

"That's because you're gone two thirds of the year, Mr. O'Tierney." Phoebe rolled her eyes. "How can you talk about that at such a time as this? I can't believe it."

Someone knocked on the door.

"You two are taking awfully long in there."

It was Dad's voice.

"One minute!" Phoebe yelled back.

"Hurry up!"

Phoebe shook her head. It seemed that wearing long sleeves and long pants might have been a mistake for this July night. "Won't we be too hot in these? I look like I'm in a wetsuit about to go scuba diving."

Fortunately, her floral linen blouse was fairly loose. She could still put the blouse over this special suit.

"What's it made of?" Phoebe zipped up her pants, and then put on her black hiking boots, which incidentally matched the catsuit.

VenomLabs never missed an opportunity to test their high-tech inventions on Mendenhall Security personnel. Mostly, they worked on AI and robotics, but every now and then a physics experiment emerged.

"A layer of non-Newtonian fluid has been woven into the fabric."

"Oh, like oobleck?" Phoebe ran her palm over her sleeves. The fabric was soft, but it also felt slightly unusual.

"Yes, but not made of cornstarch and water. This one is synthetic and waterproof. However, the concept is the same. Wear it normally, and it drapes. Hit it with a bullet, and it will harden instantly and block the bullet."

"Hence the armor. However, this won't work if the enemy takes a headshot."

"True." His voice was strained.

He sounded like he was struggling, so Phoebe turned around to see what was going on and found her husband trying to get the long sleeve over his prosthetic arm. It snagged at the elbow.

She helped him with it.

"Thanks. I can handle the rest," Keenan said. "You go outside to wait for me before your dad pitches a fit again."

"He still thinks of me as his little girl."

"I get it. No worries. I'll be out in a minute."

With three prosthetic limbs, he took more time than other people to get dressed each day. Phoebe had learned not to rush him. However, Dad hadn't understood that part of their life together.

One thing that Phoebe had learned through Keenan was patience. Now more than ever, she needed patience to wait for the auction to begin so that she could buy back her son.

That was, assuming they had really brought Jamie here tonight.

What a shame that it had to come to this. However, Phoebe was certain that when all this was over, she and Keenan would make sure it never happened again to their family and hopefully to other families as well.

CHAPTER 8

"Apart of me wishes that Noreen is at the auction house so that we could teach her a lesson once and for all." Phoebe sounded serious.

And genuinely honest.

That was one of the traits that Keenan appreciated about his wife. No sugar coating. No people pleasing.

Phoebe said what she meant. Straight from her heart.

Either you like her or you don't.

And Keenan loved her and only her. Adored her and only her.

He reached over in his seat in the van to squeeze Phoebe's hand. He would've hugged her also, but his tight safety belt said "no-no" as the van rumbled toward the north side of Peachtree City.

Long ago, when Keenan had been single and free, and doing exceptionally well in the British Special Forces, he had almost been tempted to sin by Noreen —back when she'd been Susan Atkins, seductive and sensual, and seemingly an innocent MI6 recruit who'd passed all her tests with flying colors.

The fact that Noreen had been a former FSB asset never bothered the MI6 minds because Noreen had portrayed herself as a political refugee. Esperanza even accepted Noreen as her protégé, and they were often paired in MI6 missions.

In some of these missions, Esperanza and Noreen sometimes crossed paths with Keenan, who was suave and striking—back when he had all four limbs.

However, Keenan's Christian faith forbade him from sinning against his future wife—which he hadn't known at that time. As a result, Noreen's seduction failed before it could begin. From that point on, Keenan either avoided her or made sure that he was never alone with her.

Like a parasite, Noreen lived and thrived among the elite, deepening her fake friendship with Esperanza and Mendenhall Security specialists. She hung out with them even after they had all left Her Majesty's—it was still during the reign of Queen Elizabeth II—services because Esperanza couldn't see through her schemes.

Afterwards, Noreen went rogue, breaking Esperanza's heart and wasting her effort and investment on an operative whom Esperanza had considered to be a naturally talented strategist.

In the midst of Noreen's rebellion years, she had found time to fall in love with Omar Nair, a Qatari businessman whose net worth surpassed five billion dollars, mostly amassed from oil.

Omar was already twice married, but his faith allowed him to take four concurrent wives. Noreen aimed to be his third and only wife, and began to scheme to get rid of Omar's other two wives and the three children between them.

When their deaths during a botched home invasion all pointed to Noreen as the culprit, Omar went berserk and called the police on her.

Heartbroken, Noreen faked her own death and vanished. Nine years after she had been supposedly buried, she reappeared at an old coffee shop in Bristol, England, where she'd been last seen prior to her "death."

By then, Omar had moved on, remarrying for the fourth and final time to a stunning model living in Spain. Two kids later, they made their home in both Qatar—where the kids could see their paternal grandparents—and Spain, where his wife's parents owned a restaurant in Barcelona.

Well, now Noreen was "alive again," having emerged from her self-imposed exile, and bent on exacting revenge.

Once the news got out, Omar disappeared with his wife and kids. Not even Mendenhall Security, with all of its resources and connections, could find him. He hadn't left any digital fingerprints. It would be harder—though not entirely impossible—to find him off the grid, but it would take more time.

For whatever demented reason, Noreen turned her attention to her Rolodex of old contacts, including former MI5 and MI6 agents, as well as former Special Forces soldiers, such as Keenan—who had become the target of her wrath.

"Why not come for me directly?" Keenan asked as the van stopped at a red light in Peachtree City.

Outside the van, there was hardly a vehicle nearby in the rainy night.

"Why bother my wife and kid?" Keenan continued his unanswered questions.

"To be technical, she came for your child first. Your wife is either spared or she's next." Esperanza looked far away. "Why didn't she come for me? I worked with her too."

"Because your husband is already dead, and you have no children," Keenan said. "It seems to me that she's looking to destroy families—spouses, children. That way, our grief is intensified. As for you, Espy, you're already punished, so to speak."

"I'd rather she attack me, to be honest." Esperanza shrugged. "If she kills me, what is there for me to worry about? I'll go to heaven, where my Lord and Savior is. I'll see Lamar again."

"I think she's still coming for me," Phoebe finally spoke. "Our son is the most vulnerable member of the family. Easy prey. I made a big mistake putting Jamie at Mrs. Madison's house. It's just another house in town. It's not a secure location at all. If the daycare was at Mendenhall Retreat, then Jamie would probably not have been taken."

"It's my mistake too," Keenan corrected her. "I'm the head of our household. I should've thought about my old enemies who might hurt you and Jamie just to get back at me. I've failed as a husband and father. Please forgive me."

"Please forgive me too," Phoebe said. "I didn't think it through. I wanted to help Maysie to earn some income so that she could get back on her feet and be independent of her ex-husband."

"Doesn't Mrs. Madison live one block away from Jamie's kindergarten?" Esperanza asked.

"That too. Maysie could pick up Jamie when she goes to pick up her son from the same K4 class." Phoebe sighed. "Since Jamie is the only child living with us, he sometimes gets lonely. Over at Mrs. Madison's house, he and Hanley play games and watch videos together until I pick him up after work."

Keenan nodded. "If Jamie goes with Phoebe to work, he'd have to play alone. Besides, it's only for several hours in the afternoon until we finish work."

"Don't worry," Esperanza said as the driver slammed on the van brakes. They all lurched forward a little bit, pulling the safety belts taut in their seats.

"I mean I'll fast track the daycare on site," Esperanza continued. "It's up to you to interview people for the daycare director position."

"I have some people in mind," Phoebe said. "For example, Darlene Myers, my daughter's adopted mother and a pastor's wife, has been running her church's preschool department for nearly twenty years. She'd be perfect if she agrees to move to the retreat, but that would depend on whether Pastor Daniel has heard the call of God to move to Misty Mountain. He'd have to find a job downtown somewhere."

Esperanza almost smiled. "Providentially, our retreat chapel has no pastor. Maybe it's time to upgrade from visiting speakers to a permanent preacher. What do y'all think?"

Keenan felt honored that Esperanza had asked for their opinion as well as Phoebe's regarding upper-echelon matters at the retreat. Esperanza hadn't talked about it for years, but the chapel was housed in the same cabin in which Lamar had been murdered.

No one else wanted to rent the cabin after they had scrubbed the blood off the floors. Then Esperanza decided that turning the cabin into a chapel would be a fitting reminder that life on earth was short and fleeting. People started asking about Lamar, and some non-Christians became curious about where Lamar was today.

In heaven, my friends. In heaven.

"Many of our guests go to the retreat to recover, whether from physical or mental trauma. Our doctors and nurses on call can treat physical issues, but we need a pastor who can handle spiritual issues and remind the congregation that ultimate healing comes from the Lord."

"Ten minutes away. Keeping the speed limit," the driver announced.

"Gita and Bryce should be already inside the warehouse." Esperanza called Cayson on her laptop.

It took a good minute for Cayson to respond. "Espy, they moved the auction house from Peachtree City to College Park. I just got off the phone with Gita. They just made a U-turn to get back on the highway."

"Gimme the address," Esperanza said. She then directed her driver to get back on Joel Cowan Parkway and go north. "I can't believe we're driving back toward the airport. Looks like it will take us another half an hour to get there."

"I wonder how Garrett is doing with all these sudden changes." Phoebe sounded concerned about her stepbrother.

"I'm sure he'll adjust. He's a Green Beret. Can't get more professional than that. Don't worry," Keenan assured her.

Keenan began to pray silently for the safety and security of not only the A Team heading toward the auction house ahead of them, but also for their B Team waiting for the rescue of his only child, Jamie.

Keenan's heart grew heavy as he prayed also for Jamie and Hanley and the other children abducted and about to be sold.

More than Keenan would ever be, Phoebe would be devastated if anything happened to Jamie. Knowing her personality, Keenan was certain that Phoebe would go full mama bear and hunt down Noreen and feed her to the sharks.

Wait. That would be me too. We'd both feed her to the sharks.

Keenan knew that God had a special punishment for those who hurt children, but he worried that the justice cited in Luke 17:2 might not happen as soon as he'd want it.

It would be better for him if a millstone were hung around his neck, and he were thrown into the sea, than that he should offend one of these little ones.

At this point, Keenan couldn't hate Noreen more for not repenting of the errors of her ways. She was the criminal, not the heroic vigilante that she was portraying herself to be.

Then again, who was Keenan to exact punish-ment on others for their wrongs against him and his family? Romans 12:19 reminded him that vengeance belonged to God.

> *Beloved, do not avenge yourselves, but rather give place to wrath; for it is written, "Vengeance is Mine, I will repay," says the Lord.*

Keenan prayed for peace in his own heart as well as in Phoebe's heart. When he had nothing more to pray at that minute, he opened his eyes only to find that Phoebe was fast asleep.

Good.

He had been worried that she'd be up all night and would be dysfunctional. At least now she could get half an hour of sleep. She wasn't a night owl like Keenan. She preferred to wake up when the sun rose. She operated at peak capacity in the daytime when the sun was in the sky.

Like clockwork, she'd be asleep by ten o'clock at night. Except tonight. It was past midnight now, long after her bedtime.

If Keenan could carry her burdens for her, he would at the drop of a hat.

So far, Phoebe had been calm and almost as cool as a cucumber. She hadn't fallen apart yet—although Keenan hadn't been there at the Tennessee pig farm to witness whether it was truly Joe who had dealt all the blows found on Newell Greer.

Yes, he would've liked to have been there to see Phoebe's demeanor when she and Joe "interrogated" Newell, the linchpin in the kidnapping case.

Without Newell's phone evidence and saved messages, none of them would've made the clear-path connection to Noreen, wherever she might be hiding. Even though the bulk of that work had been done by Dmitri's team at Still Salvage, the enhancement had come from Binary Systems.

Havilah and Asher had pointed to Peachtree City as a general location, but Cayson and Iseul pinpointed a longitude and latitude. Furthermore, they had tracked the schedule and location changes.

How? Keenan knew it was best not to ask unnecessary questions. All he needed to know was where to find his son.

"It would be easier if Noreen also shows up at the auction house," Keenan said aloud for Esperanza to hear.

"But we know that's not her style," Esperanza replied. "That mastermind doesn't want to get her hands stained. The dirty work will always be done by someone else."

Keenan nodded. "We know her pattern. When she went after Omar's wives and kids, nothing could be linked to her. If not for her slip of the tongue in front of Omar, she would've gotten away scot-free."

"And would've remained free to walk the streets even if she hadn't pretended to be dead," Esperanza said.

"Why would she take a redundant step?" Phoebe asked with bleary eyes.

"Did I wake you up?" Keenan asked gently. "Sorry I didn't whisper."

"It's okay." Phoebe shifted in her seat. She massaged a shoulder and then the other. "I'm glad I woke up. I didn't want to fall asleep and be left behind when we get there. Speaking of which, are we there yet?"

Keenan shook his head. "No. They moved the auction house to College Park so we're still driving."

"I heard that part before I fell asleep. Do you know why they did that at the last minute? Was our intel bad?"

"I don't know." It was the truth. Sometimes Keenan walked into a mission shrouded with fog. He prayed that his extensive training would come through so that he could handle any situation.

"If they knew we knew..." Phoebe began to say.

"Or if they have a mole inside the FBI..." Esperanza's voice trailed off.

"Speaking of whom, have we contacted the FBI about the auction house?" Phoebe asked.

"They already knew about it," Cayson's voice came through the laptop speakers. "I also told them about the change of venue, but they already have undercover agents and informants inside the auction house."

Keenan had no idea Cayson had been listening.

"Then will we be interfering in their raid?" Phoebe asked. "I worry about Jamie's safety."

"No. We're operating independently." It was all Esperanza said.

Keenan felt better that law enforcement was on the way or already inside.

"Did you tell them that we're attending the auction?" Keenan asked.

"No." Esperanza didn't explain her reasons.

She handed out bottles of water instead. They were ice cold and hit the spot. Keenan noticed that

Phoebe drank up the entire bottle without saying a word. Normally, she wouldn't drink water from a plastic bottle because she was afraid of ingesting microplastics.

However, this time she hadn't had time to pack a picnic basket.

Keenan prayed again as they approached College Park. Overhead, a Boeing 747 descended, no doubt heading for Hartsfield.

Esperanza's phone rang. "Hey Gita. Are you there yet?"

Suddenly she sat up straight. "What?"

Her face paled. She tapped the speaker button on her phone. "Garrett, say that again so that we can all hear it."

"We're not quite in College Park yet, but we got in a wreck," Garrett said. "A tractor trailer jackknifed in the rain. Five-car pileup. We're in the middle of this mess."

"Oh no!" Jerome suddenly yelled from the backseat. So far, he had been listening without commenting.

"Are you okay?" Phoebe asked.

"I'm fine, Sis. No worries. The fire trucks just arrived, and they're extracting Gita and Bryce from the front seat. I was in the backseat with the briefcase, and narrowly missed getting my legs crushed."

"Thank God you made it out," Phoebe said. "Can you tell us what Gita's and Bryce's conditions are?"

"They're still alive, but they're bleeding a lot, though not too serious. The Bentley is built like a tank and protected us." Garrett paused, as if wondering how much more to say without making his stepsister worry unnecessarily. "The ambulance is here. Paramedics on the scene. I'm going to assume they'll take them to the nearest hospital with a Level One trauma center, and that would be Grady."

The Grady Memorial Hospital was another twenty minutes away from College Park.

"They're loading Gita and Bryce into the ambulance. I'm going with them to Grady, okay?"

"Garrett, have them look you over too," Phoebe said.

"Just in case of internal injuries," Jerome chimed in.

"Don't worry. The armored catsuit did help some when parts of it stiffened around me. Overall, God protected us. We're still alive."

"Thank God." Jerome settled down.

"The weather doesn't help. It's still raining, and it's making the highway slippery," Garrett added.

"We'll keep the same hourly rate, Garrett," Esperanza said.

"I'm not concerned about the pay," Garrett replied. "But the briefcase..."

Yes, the briefcase filled with stacks of hundred dollar bills amounting to a million dollars. The human auction only dealt with cash and gold bars.

Esperanza had prepared two briefcases. She had given one to Gita. The other briefcase filled with a million dollars worth of gold bars was with Esperanza in the van.

Keenan wondered if they might use less than two million dollars to buy back two kids. Then again, who could tell what greedy criminals would charge?

In any case, they would try to reclaim as many kids as they could with the two million dollars in total.

When the FBI raided the auction house, they might get their money back. Or not.

"I'm going to send Leilani to Grady to meet you and take the briefcase from you," Esperanza said. "She will drive to our van and give me the briefcase."

Leilani was another new hire at the Mendenhall Security branch in Atlanta. She was primarily Esperanza's assistant, helping her plan her schedule and meetings all week long. However, she used to be a civilian cryptologist in the US Navy, so Keenan was sure that Esperanza would tap into that skillset soon enough.

"And how much time will that add?" Garrett asked.

"She's working late at our office in Alpharetta," Esperanza said. "It'll take her about forty minutes or more to get to Grady. Then it will take her another twenty minutes to get to me."

"May I suggest an alternative idea?" Garrett asked over the phone.

"Sure." Esperanza didn't hesitate in replying.

"How about I don't go to the hospital? Gita and Bryce are in good hands. Nothing I can do at the hospital," Garrett said. "So how about I wait for you here by the roadside? You can pick me up since you're sure to pass by this wreckage. I'll hand you the briefcase and also go with y'all."

Keenan was glad that Garrett hadn't said words he shouldn't say in public as he made the phone call. Even though Gita's phone was encrypted, the fact that Garrett had to speak in front of the victims and first responders meant that he wasn't in a secure location to speak in the first place.

"What if you're more seriously injured than you think?" Jerome's voice was tinged with concern.

"I don't think so," Garrett said. "I have some bruises and some small cuts, but I wore my safety belt, you know. I didn't bounce around."

"Good." Jerome was visibly relieved.

"When this is over, I'll go see my doctor and have a check-up, okay?" Garrett said.

"Promise?" Phoebe asked.

"Yes, Sis." Garrett emphasized "Sis," most likely for Phoebe's benefit.

Keenan was happy to hear him call his stepsister "Sis." From an abandoned orphan to being adopted into Jerome's family to having four siblings in a blended family, Phoebe had come a very long way.

"In any case, I'm thankful to God that you're alive, Garrett—all three of you," Phoebe said.

"Okay, Garrett. I'll take your idea over mine. Let's pick you up on our way to College Park. Just remember your promise to your sister to see a doctor after this is over." Esperanza showed another leadership trait of hers: teachability. Her willingness to learn gave her employees opportunities to shine, and when they shone, she also shone.

"We're five minutes from the wreck," the van driver told Esperanza.

That meant that they had a way to go before they reached College Park. It was starting to make Keenan worry that they'd miss the auction.

"Standby, Garrett." Esperanza ended the call.

Just as quickly, she speed-dialed Leilani and

instructed her to hop in her car and drive to Grady to take care of Gita and Bryce.

After the call, Esperanza turned to Keenan and Phoebe. "Houston, we have a problem."

"What?" Phoebe asked.

"We've just lost our A Team."

Phoebe nodded. "But your B Team is suited up."

Keenan stared at Phoebe.

"Espy could be the buyer. I'll be her assistant." Phoebe pointed to Keenan. "You and Garrett can be our bodyguards. You two carry one briefcase each. I have faith in God that He'll use you two to shield us— or better phrased, that He'll use all four of us to protect Jamie."

"Didn't they say that no weapons are allowed in?" Keenan asked.

"As far as I know." Phoebe nodded. "Then the only way people could hurt us is using things like sticks and stones—unless they smuggled in a firearm or a blade."

"Another thing. We can't stop this van in front of the strip mall without arousing suspicion," Esperanza said.

"Is there anyone in town you can call who can lend us a vehicle? I don't think it has to be as expensive as the Bentley that the A Team wrecked."

Esperanza made a face. "That's an expensive rental, but the lives inside are priceless, so I'm glad they made it out alive."

"So we need to rent a new vehicle," Phoebe said.

Esperanza nodded. She called Leilani again to make arrangements for a vehicle to be delivered to them five blocks away from the new auction venue.

After Esperanza finished calling, she still looked worried. "The whole idea was not to show our faces. Noreen knows what Keenan and I look like, and no doubt what you look like too, Phoebe."

"It's too late for silicon masks even if Leilani could bring them from the supply closet," Keenan said.

"No, they'll notice us right away since we'll be up close with the other buyers—especially if we sweat like pigs." Esperanza thought for a second. "Cayson, you have any idea?"

"We cannot jam the communication all around the building because it would hinder the FBI," Cayson said. "Remember that they also have under-cover agents inside who need to communicate with their ground commander."

"But if we don't, Noreen can observe us remote-ly," Keenan said. "Assuming she's not in town in person."

"We don't have to block every internet feed going outside," Phoebe said. "Maybe we just need to block non-FBI livestreams going out."

"I'm afraid Binary Systems can't do any of that—officially," Cayson said. "Any interference could be problematic. I don't want to be summoned to court."

Officially?

Keenan caught the word, and apparently so did Phoebe. She shook her head at Esperanza.

"Thank you, Cayson," Esperanza said. "I'll check in with you as soon as we park near the auction house."

After Cayson was offline, Esperanza turned to Phoebe. "I know that you want to say something."

"Maybe we don't need to block anything," Phoebe

suggested. "We need to find someone to monitor all Wi-Fi going in and out of the auction house, paying careful attention to outgoing livestreams."

"Good idea," Esperanza said. "If we can monitor the streams going in and out, maybe we can track down Noreen's point of origin. She's brazen enough that she's probably watching the auction live with a feeling of schadenfreude."

"I suspect she will be," Keenan said. "She has always been like that. She likes to watch her handiwork and keep tabs on the progress."

"Sounds like you know Noreen very well." Phoebe raised her eyebrows at Keenan.

"Uh, yes. I wanted to tell you more when we were still in Peachtree City, but didn't have the opportunity," Keenan said. "I worked with Noreen closely for a while. She wanted to date me, but I said no."

"Just like that?" Phoebe asked. "Weren't you tempted?"

"What's the point of it when her heart is evil?" Those words simply spilled out of Keenan's lips. He waited to see Phoebe's reaction.

"Enough about the past," Esperanza reminded everyone. "We have a present problem. Cayson can't help us beyond what he has already done."

"Yeah. We're no longer asking him to jam the internet connections all around the building, but to scan them instead," Phoebe said. "Such a thing is illegal in all fifty states. We might run afoul of privacy and wiretap laws."

"Unless the FBI does it themselves. They can get a search warrant," Keenan added.

"However, if we tell them we're here, we might be barred from going in," Esperanza said.

"If we don't tell them, they will think that we have no confidence in law enforcement," Jerome finally said.

He'd been sitting in the van without speaking much, except for the short exchange with Garrett earlier.

Sitting next to him, Joe hadn't said a word either. In fact, he was on his laptop the entire drive. What was he up to? Keenan didn't have time to ask him.

Finally, Joe looked up. "I took care of it for you, Espy."

"What?" Esperanza's eyes grew big.

"I called Dmitri and updated him on what's going on."

"Dmitri?" The last person to cross Keenan's mind. He didn't know what to say. He didn't want Mendenhall Security to get into trouble with the FBI for skirting around them to get help from such a figure as Dmitri, with his mysterious past and dubious present.

Then again, Dmitri had fewer red tapes than Cayson and way more connections than Esperanza.

Perhaps Dmitri was the trump card.

"No need to thank me," Joe said to Esperanza. "Just add it to my Christmas bonus. I take cold, hard cash in unmarked bills."

"I didn't tell you to call Dmitri," Esperanza said.

"No, you didn't. I did it on my own accord." Joe didn't seem to care that he'd defied his boss. "While y'all talk about legal hurdles, the lives of two four-year-olds are at stake."

Esperanza grunted. "If you get arrested, you're fired, and I don't know you."

Keenan glanced at Phoebe. He wanted to tell her that, as the deputy director, Phoebe would be working for such a boss. It wasn't too late to bail out now.

Phoebe didn't seem bothered by what Esperanza just said to Joe. Perhaps Phoebe knew Esperanza more than Keenan did.

"We're here," the van driver announced.

"Let's go," Esperanza snapped.

CHAPTER 9

By the time they reached the strip mall in their rented second Bentley, a large crowd had formed at the entrance of the dinky nightclub with its half broken neon sign nailed on top of a previous sign above the front entrance.

Through her smart glasses, Phoebe could see a faded soot outline under the neon sight. It seemed to spell the previous name of the establishment. Neither nightclub names appealed to her, but that wasn't why she was here.

On both sides of the nightclub were shops with welded steel bars across their windows. One of them was a pawn shop with the words "We Buy Gold" emblazoned above the door. Another was a smoke shop with a faded metal poster of a Cuban cigar.

These two shops, as well as the others along the entire strip mall, were all closed and padlocked. However, the parking lot was full in front of those shops. Phoebe guessed that they might be all clubbers.

Keenan made two turns in the mall parking lot

and returned to the nightclub when he saw a parking spot open up. Unfortunately, it was taken.

"I'm surprised there's no valet parking here." Esperanza adjusted her tortoiseshell smart glasses over her nose.

"I hear you, Espy. On my way."

Joe's voice came through on the built-in headset on Phoebe's eyeglass temple tips that rested over her ears.

"On your way to where?" Espy asked.

Joe didn't reply. All they heard was some sort of engine. Revving engine.

Esperanza turned to Phoebe. "When Joe trains you to be my deputy director, please don't pick up his maverick habits. Check with me before you do anything crazy."

"You mean like contacting Dmitri?" Phoebe asked.

"That and more. Oh the headaches he gives me sometimes." Esperanza shook her head. "You never know what he drags into the office. I expanded my legal team just for him."

Phoebe already knew all that about Joe, and she still liked the former soldier. If not for him, they'd never have made it this far in such a short amount of time.

Looking out from her side window, Phoebe saw that the nightclub patrons wore all sorts of outfits, from shimmering to velvet, from low cut necklines to mini skirts. They looked somewhat dressy.

"Will our diving suits fit in?" Phoebe laughed.

"Catsuits," Esperanza corrected her.

"What does VenomLabs call these?"

"It's still experimental. Right now there's a debate in their design team. Some want to keep the generic 'armored catsuits.' That seems cartoony, but nobody asked me."

"As long as it does its job," Garrett said.

He was sitting in the passenger seat, and Keenan in the driver's seat. Garrett had offered to drive, but Esperanza vetoed it because he'd just been in a wreck.

Both of them had worn halfway decent jackets over their armored catsuits.

Esperanza had thrown her usual leather jacket over her catsuit, and she looked like a model with her sleek pulled-back jet black hair and hardly any makeup. She looked like she could fill the cover of a fashion magazine and start a worldwide movement for forty-something women.

As for Phoebe, she neither had the height nor the right weight ratio to match Esperanza's smooth almond skin. Her skin was sometimes blotchy due to stress and a lack of sleep, and sometimes itchy due to...yes, stress and a lack of sleep.

All she had on was her floral linen blouse, the same shirt she'd worn back in Tennessee, at work all day at the retreat, then in the hospital visiting Mrs. Madison, and then at the pig farm wrestling Newell to the ground.

Truth be told, she hadn't expected to leave the mountain at all, let alone fly out of state to Georgia to this seedy side of College Park. She'd done it to rescue her son, not to parade on the catwalk.

Still, she had to get inside the nightclub.

"I'm dressed for the warehouse." Phoebe chuckled.

To Keenan's credit, he didn't say a word. If he'd said something like, "You look good in anything," he'd be lying through his teeth.

As Keenan was still looking for a parking space, Phoebe thought about her attire. Her blouse was for day wear. Right now she had worn it over her catsuit. How could she dress it up?

She could tie the blouse around her waist like a sash, but then wouldn't it draw too much attention to the catsuit itself? She didn't want her floral fabric to make her waist look wider.

Then again, this wasn't the time to worry about looks. She just needed to fit into the nightclub crowd.

To be honest, the matte-black catsuit didn't have any shimmering exterior. It had been made for one faction only: to stop bullets. Its non-Newtonian properties hadn't been tested in public.

At night, black blended into the surroundings.

Phoebe thought of another idea. She unbuttoned her blouse and took it off. Putting it on her lap, she folded it into various geometric shapes until she found a style that made the blouse long enough to wrap around her neck like a scarf or shawl. She twisted a part of the blouse until she could tie a reef knot over one collar bone, letting the floral design of the blouse drape over the other shoulder.

"Okay?" Phoebe asked Esperanza.

"Wow." Her boss smiled. "You need to do my wardrobe. You seem to be natural at styling."

"Desperate is more like it." Phoebe looked out the window again.

Keenan was still driving up and down, looking for a parking space.

"I was going to suggest that maybe Keenan could drop us off first, but he can't." Phoebe sighed. "We only have one QR code and it's with Espy. If Keenan doesn't come with us at the same time, he might not be able to get in at all."

If not for Dmitri's intel—all thanks to Joe in the van two blocks from here—they wouldn't have known that the ticket into the auction room was a special QR code that Dmitri had to give them. Once the bouncer scanned it, that would be all it took.

No one would ask them to open the briefcase to check the goods. If they had no money to pay, then they would sacrifice their lives and become more victims of the human traffickers. It was that simple.

Phoebe heard the rumbling first before she saw the single light coming toward their Bentley. The Harley-Davidson *Nightster Special* growled to a rumbling idle next to the driver's side.

"Who's that?" Garrett looked worried. "Are these windows made of ballistic glass?"

No one answered him.

"Joe, is that you?" Esperanza asked through her smart glasses.

Phoebe thought it was Joe but she couldn't see his face due to the helmet he was wearing. Also, it looked like he had also rented a leather jacket to go with his Harley. It made Joe appear bigger than his five-foot-six frame. He had said that he'd been taller back when he was in the service, but as he grew older, he started to slouch or something.

"Yeah, it's me, Joe, your personal valet." He saluted and revved his engine for good measure. "I saw a motorcycle parking spot back there. Follow me.

I'll take the car. Please add the valet tip to my Christmas bonus, Espy."

"Remind me again why you have the highest health insurance plan in my entire organization." Esperanza laughed as Keenan waited for Joe to ride ahead of their car, escorting them around the block once.

Joe parked his Harley, got off, staggered a bit on account of his bad knee, and removed his helmet.

Keenan stopped the car closer to the Harley so that other vehicles could pass by. He got out of the car and squeezed in the backseat, pushing Phoebe to the middle in between him and Esperanza.

"I gather you work out," Phoebe teased as her left arm touched her husband's right arm with its thick biceps.

"I gather you work out too." Keenan flashed her a smile.

Esperanza rolled her eyes. "You two. I can't even..."

Joe put on his safety belt and drove the Bentley thirty feet to the front entrance of the nightclub. He literally stopped the car without caring if anyone else was behind him.

"Joe, you're a hero," Phoebe said.

Joe might not have heard her, but Phoebe didn't repeat herself.

He was busy navigating the Bentley among jaywalkers who didn't care that a five-thousand-pound bulldozer was coming their way.

Joe slowed down near the entrance of the night-club, but he couldn't get any closer on account of the crowd.

"Get out quickly before someone honks at me," Joe ordered his passengers. "I don't like people honking at me, especially when I'm driving the getaway car."

"I'll call you when we're done," Esperanza said.

"Sounds good."

"But wait for a minute to make sure we get inside. I don't know if the QR code works."

"Wave to me when you clear security."

"Thank you, Joe." Esperanza said it first, but all of them chimed in.

Phoebe followed Esperanza closely, letting her go first since she had the QR code to get past the bouncer. Keenan and Garrett, each carrying a suitcase, brought up the flank.

The QR code cleared without any issue. Esperanza still waved to Joe even though Joe's smart glasses clearly transmitted the entire conversation that Esperanza had with the bouncer.

The group of four people made it inside the dark and noisy hall. Some sort of emo rap or pop punk music blasted from the speakers all around them in the room.

Phoebe wished she had worn ear plugs.

Her eyes watered in the thick smoke shrouding her as they were escorted to the inner sanctum of the nightclub. The DJ wearing a tall hat danced a bit, and a mini light show strobed around his hat.

There were no other lights, and Phoebe couldn't see where she was stepping if not for the smart glasses showing her the way forward in infrared.

She was thankful that she'd worn closed-toe boots because she was shuffling forward and feeling her way on the dark floor. Her smart glasses made sure she could see fine, but she was concerned about the crowd itself that didn't have such glasses.

Every now and then, sprightly dancers almost bumped into her, but Keenan's swift prosthetic arm pushed them away.

Phoebe kept moving, following Esperanza forward as the lights above them grew dimmer.

The DJ played a new song and raised the volume. The noise level was deafening, and Phoebe found herself unable to think. She tried her best to mentally block out the cacophony as well as people shouting and yelling above the noise to one another.

Drinks spilled all around her. The smell of sweat and smoke and spirits nearly made her faint.

Wait a minute. Smoke?

Wasn't smoking banned in all nightclubs in metro Atlanta? Well, maybe this nightclub hadn't gotten the memo from a decade ago.

Phoebe lifted a part of her blouse tied around her neck and covered her nose and mouth with it. She could breathe just a little better, but better nonetheless.

It looked like she had found two uses for her blouse just tonight alone.

If only the armored catsuit also came with accessories such as a face mask, a ballistic baseball hat, or something for the head and face. Oh, and gloves for the hands too, just in case. Maybe they needed to make armored shoes as well.

Phoebe made a mental note to add her suggestions when she filled out the product evaluation for VenomLabs.

Their usher stopped at a locked door, painted all black. Here, the lighting was fairly good, and Phoebe didn't have to use the infrared feature on her smart glasses.

She talked to the man sitting at a barstool by the door. He didn't look very comfortable, but next to him was what looked like a mail box set into the wall.

"One hundred thousand, please."

He was polite. Phoebe would give him that.

Otherwise, he looked downright bored.

Just then, Phoebe noticed that he was wearing bright orange foam earplugs. Even this guard couldn't stand the noise.

"What do you mean?" Esperanza asked.

"That's the entry fee to the auction," the usher explained with a smile.

"Per person," the guard added. He must have lip-read the usher, or perhaps the foam earplugs were useless.

"Four hundred thousand dollars then," Esperanza said.

Phoebe wondered how this was going to work out. Esperanza only had two million dollars in the brief-cases. If she handed this guard four hundred thousand dollars in cash from the briefcase, she might not have enough left for the auction if the bids went high.

Phoebe and Keenan only wore their wedding bands that were not worth much if sold—although their sentimental values were priceless.

Esperanza reached under her collar and pulled out her diamond necklace, the very one that she had kept all these years since Lamar had passed away.

"No..." Phoebe reached for her shoulder.

Esperanza lifted the diamond pendant so that the guard could see. "Last week, I had this Tiffany diamond necklace appraised. It's worth six hundred thousand dollars. Will you take it as the entrance fee?"

Whoa.

Phoebe was visibly moved that her boss would sacrifice her treasured gift to rescue Jamie.

The guard removed an earplug from one ear. "I don't have a jewelry appraiser on standby. I'll take cash or gold only."

"All right. Half and half, okay?" Esperanza pushed her diamond necklace under her collar.

"Suit yourself."

Esperanza nodded to Keenan and Garrett.

"I'll call Leilani now to see if she has more cash and gold," Joe said in each of their smart glasses.

Obviously, none of them could reply to Joe. But Phoebe knew that Esperanza didn't have an endless supply of liquid cash or gold. Some of her assets were in trust funds that could not be accessed. Plus, she had multi-million-dollar projects to fund.

If they didn't rescue Jamie tonight, Mendenhall Security might not be able to do any more for them if this search-and-rescue operation went on and on ad infinitum.

Phoebe also realized that if the FBI arrived—soon, hopefully—the money might still be intact. However, if they arrived too soon, the human traffickers might disappear with the kids to who knew where.

The guard gladly accepted the two hundred thousand dollars in cash and another two hundred in gold bars. He put the entrance fee into the mail slot on the wall, and pushed a button, which opened a door.

Inside, the air was stale. The air conditioner was not on full blast, and there were no windows. Phoebe lifted more of her blouse to cover her nose, layering the fabric around her face.

Immediately, Phoebe's eyes went to the stage up against one wall. It was tall enough for her to see who was on the platform.

Five emaciated children between the ages of eight and ten, all with terrified looks in their eyes, stood in a row. Chained to one another, they were crying and shaking uncontrollably, rattling the chains.

Phoebe's knees buckled. She leaned against Keenan, who held her up.

"I'm okay," she whispered.

No, I'm not. But I have to be.

She scanned each of the children's faces, wanting to remember what they looked like. She prayed for them silently, asking God to rescue them.

The auctioneer held a microphone. "One million! Going once, going twice! Sold to Paddle 98!"

The kids were herded off the stage. Soft music started playing while they prepared the next batch of kids.

There were no chairs anywhere in the room. A bunch of bidders stood in the open space in front of a platform. They came in all shapes and sizes, and all ethnicities. None of them talked to one another, so Phoebe wasn't able to guess where they might have originated.

Who on earth would buy trafficked children?

This world in which Phoebe lived was spiraling

down to the pits. What could she do about it? Perhaps doing the best she could at Mendenhall Retreat, serving heroes and their families, would be her contribution to a better world.

And yes, she could pray for God to deliver the world from sin. It was a big prayer, but her God is the Lord of the universe, as she had read often in Revelation 1:8.

"I am the Alpha and the Omega, the Beginning and the End," says the Lord, "who is and who was and who is to come, the Almighty."

The next batch of minors looked like teenagers. All three girls had matted hair. Looking drowsy or perhaps drugged, they staggered onto the stage. They were chained together around their waists. Duct tape over their mouths prevented them from calling for help.

Phoebe felt lightheaded, but it quickly passed.

"You okay?" Garrett whispered in her ear.

Phoebe nodded.

Esperanza turned to check on her. Her brown Spanish eyes flared. She was angry—probably angry enough to do something drastic.

Phoebe wanted to cheer her on, but she remained quiet.

"Pray," Keenan whispered in her other ear.

"I did," she whispered back.

Waiting between the batches of kids dragged onto the stage made Phoebe anxious. She could tell that Keenan wanted to hold her hand but didn't want to arouse suspicion.

The routine was the same. A door opened on one side of the stage, the kids were dragged onto the platform, sold, and then taken across the stage to the other side, exiting via a small door there. They were followed by their buyers with cash or gold in hand.

The bids had been very high so far, but business was business to these human traffickers.

After a while, Phoebe wanted to sit down, but there was nowhere to sit. Then the entry door opened again.

And she saw her son.

CHAPTER 10

There he was, standing right in the middle among five disheveled boys.

He had a black eye, but as clear as day, that was Jamie. Phoebe could spot the cowlick on top of his head anywhere. A tuft of hair stuck out of it—reminding her of the cartoon character, Dennis the Menace.

Chained to the boy in front and behind him, Jamie limped forward, dragging a foot that had a dirty bandage around the ankle. They hadn't even bothered to replace the shoes he'd left behind at Mrs. Madison's house.

Phoebe's eyes blurred. She winced and blinked a couple of times. She stared at the boy behind Jamie again to make sure she hadn't made a mistake.

The boy glanced back, and Phoebe recognized the kid as Hanley. One of Hanley's eyes was swollen so badly it was almost shut.

Phoebe felt sorry for him that he'd also been beaten, like Jamie. Perhaps she felt even sorrier for Hanley because it had been his own father, that no-good Newell Greer, who had sold his own son into modern-day slavery.

How could human auctions be a thing at all in the twenty-first century? It was beyond belief.

The traffickers yelled at the boys to move faster.

Jamie's lips curled as he made a valiant effort to comply.

Yes, that's my son, Jamie.

Phoebe reached out to grab Keenan's hand and realized they had both done so at the same time. They exchanged knowing glances before dropping their arms to their sides.

Phoebe nudged Esperanza. The latter nodded slightly. She had seen Jamie too.

Phoebe prayed for success. They needed to rescue both Jamie and Hanley. Whether one or the other, they had to purchase all five boys.

This was it. Would they have enough money to come through?

The bids began.

Phoebe prayed and tried to remain calm. Her hands were sweating. She felt like she was going to pass out after seeing her own son on the auction block. It didn't help that she found it hard to breathe in this poorly ventilated room.

The auctioneer switched languages easily from English to Spanish and then back again.

Bilingual Esperanza kept up without any problem.

"I've got 750. Do I hear 760? How about 770? Anyone?" He pointed to a paddle in the crowd. "Who will give me 780?"

Esperanza also raised her paddle.

The auction chants continued.

Standing there, Phoebe's knees wobbled again. She made another mental note to be disciplined about exercising every day from now on. Even in her late thirties, she was feeling unfit.

Then again, this was traumatizing for her.

Once again, Keenan was there to prop her up, literally.

She straightened up. "I'm okay."

By the time she refocused her attention back to the auctioneer, the bids had escalated.

"Nine hundred thousand, ladies and gentlemen," the auctioneer announced. "Who's in at 920? 930?"

The price went up, up, up.

Whoa. What is happening?

Esperanza glanced over to the other side of the room to find her opponent in the bidding war.

On stage, one of the kids collapsed. It wasn't Jamie or Hanley, but since they were all chained together, they all fell down.

Phoebe nearly lunged forward to run up on the stage, but Keenan pulled her back with his robotic prosthetic hand that was too strong for her to fight off.

The traffickers, looking jaded, simply left the kids sitting down on the floor.

"Do I hear 990?" The auctioneer nodded. "One million dollars?"

Esperanza's paddle went up.

They had the money, but Joe better bring more, just in case.

Phoebe realized then that Joe couldn't get in without the single-use QR code. Perhaps one of them had to go outside of the building to get the money from him—if it had to come to that.

A kid who had been sitting up keeled over.

The bidders gasped.

"Is this a runt litter?" someone asked in a heavy accent of some sort.

Beads of sweat formed on Phoebe's forehead and flowed down her face onto her makeshift mask. Inside the suit, she was feeling hot, like she was in a sauna at the gym.

With two kids out cold on stage, there was little chance another person would outbid Esperanza. Her paddle was still up in the air.

"One million now," the auctioneer said. "Looking for one million one hundred thousand. Anyone? Bid now. One-one!"

Esperanza lifted her paddle even higher.

"We have one-one. Who'll give me one-two?"

No one.

Not a single one.

"All right, folks." The auctioneer scanned the room. "One-one. Going once, going twice. Sold!"

So they bought Jamie back for one million one hundred thousand dollars.

Three walking kids, including Jamie and Hanley, were led off the stage, while two men carried the unconscious remaining two kids.

Their chains clanging ever louder in Phoebe's ears.

Phoebe almost ran ahead of Esperanza, but she stopped herself. This wasn't the time to panic or do something out of the ordinary. She stepped back and let the calm and cool Esperanza go first. Keenan and Garrett made sure that the jostling crowd didn't push though the exit door they were meant to walk through.

On the other side of the wall, it was mass chaos. Kids were crying as they were herded out by their buyers. Some cried "mommy" in several languages. No one responded to them.

Phoebe wanted to go hug every single one of them and find their mothers for them, but first she had to rescue Jamie.

Corralled at a corner, the five kids sat down on the floor. The two kids who had passed out on stage had somehow been revived. Their eyes were vacant, and they stared ahead.

They all looked hungry and traumatized. After this was over, they would need counseling and prayer and a whole lot of tender, loving care to nurse them back to normal health.

Phoebe dropped down on her knees in front of Jamie and hugged him tightly. She started to cry.

"Mommy?" Jamie whispered in her ear and nuzzled her scarf.

"Shhhh. Hide-and-seek." Jamie and Keenan had played this game before where they had to hide quietly so that they wouldn't be found. Phoebe had avoided the game altogether, but now it would come in handy. "Keep quiet."

"Okay." His eyes lit up.

Phoebe let him go and stood up.

Jamie and Hanley both clutched to her legs, one each.

But first, she had to get Jamie out of this place.

The worst was not over yet until they left this auction house and secured some police protection.

Esperanza handed over the hundred dollar bills and gold bars, leaving only half a million dollars worth of gold in the briefcase.

Once the payment had exchanged hands, Esperanza asked for the chains to be removed from the kids. A man came with a bolt cutter and started the work, but the first freed kid jumped up, screamed, and ran away.

Garrett chased after him and brought him back, and hushed him so that they wouldn't attract attention that they couldn't afford.

They couldn't make a scene until they left the building.

How could they get these kids out safely? Phoebe realized that they hadn't thought that far.

She looked around to see how other people were transporting the kids out of the room. Some had brought wheeled utility bins and put all the kids in them. It was the weirdest thing Phoebe had seen, but it seemed to work.

"Keep going," Esperanza ordered the man with the bolt cutter. "Cut the chains."

When all five boys were separated, Phoebe lifted Jamie off his feet and carried him in front, putting his legs around her waist and his arms around her neck.

"Hold on tight," Phoebe said. "And be quiet, okay?"

He nodded his head on Phoebe's neck and hugged her even more tightly.

Keenan lifted Hanley with one arm because he still carried the rest of the gold in the briefcase.

Nearby, Garrett picked up two kids, leaving the skinniest kid for Esperanza.

Phoebe knew that Garrett had done that on purpose, but he probably didn't know that Esperanza was the strongest woman in her age group that Phoebe knew.

They made their way to the "Exit" sign, which hopefully would lead them to freedom. In spite of the atrocity, the auction had gone well—

"Stop."

It was the same guard.

"Didn't we pay you earlier?" Esperanza asked.

"This is the exit toll."

"The what?" Esperanza drew a deep breath. "How much?"

"What remains in that briefcase." He pointed to Keenan's burden.

"All I have left are gold bars." Esperanza stepped closer and lowered her voice.

The guard motioned for Keenan to drop the briefcase in front of him.

"Open it," he said.

"We have no available hands," Esperanza said. "How about you open it? Take what you want."

As the man knelt on the floor to open the briefcase, Phoebe thought she could take him out. However, they were in enemy territory and could not escape if they created a ruckus.

Their most important task right now was to leave this place.

Esperanza nodded to her B Team—which was practically their new A Team—and they all stepped back.

As soon as the man opened the briefcase, a puff of smoke came out, and a small explosion sent the man flying back.

The room erupted in screams. People scrambled for cover as more white smoke came out of the brief-case, filling the room.

"Let's go!" Esperanza said.

Phoebe hugged Jamie tightly and ran toward the exit. Her smart glasses adjusted to the smoke-filled room and showed her the clear path out.

She heard someone shout "Fire!" behind her, followed by a stampede.

It was obviously a false alarm, but people must've panicked. Somewhere, a fire alarm actually went off—perhaps someone had pulled it—and the doors flung open to the cloudy summer night.

"Where's the FBI?" Phoebe asked.

Didn't they know to come here, to this auction house?

Their rental Bentley came screeching to a halt in front of them, but before they could pile in, sirens blared all around them and lights flashed.

Police vehicles, SWAT vans, and federal agents in Kevlar vests and weapons drawn swarmed the side of the building.

Esperanza ordered her team all to get down on the sidewalk and wait. A couple of police officers guarded all nine of them, plus Joe in the car. He was ordered out of the car and onto the sidewalk.

Jamie shivered in Phoebe's arms, but she did not allow him to look at the building. He faced the Bentley while she faced the building.

Phoebe and Keenan exchanged glances, but neither said a word.

Phoebe watched the FBI agents enter the building. Smoke had somewhat cleared inside, and the ceiling lights showed a chaotic scene as the FBI agents rounded up people.

"Thank you for coming," Esperanza said to the police officer nearest her. "What took you so long?"

He didn't answer.

"Because there are multiple auction houses across the city at the same time."

A familiar voice.

Everyone turned toward the street.

Tall, bearded, and smiling, he looked good at his age.

"Dmitri!" Esperanza gasped.

He nodded to the police officer.

"I came all the way down the mountain to make sure you were okay." Dmitri waved to his old friends.

"Are we that important to you?" Esperanza asked.

"Not really." Dmitri grinned. "I happened to be in town when Joe called me. I cannot believe you went in yourselves. Do you know how dangerous it is, little children?"

"I'm sorry, Grandpa." Esperanza hung her head.

"It's a good thing you're not my real daughter or else I'd ground you right now." He nodded at Keenan and Garrett.

Dmitri stared straight at Phoebe. "You owe me dinner, young mother."

"Any time, Dmitri. Thank you very much." Phoebe's voice cracked.

"You're very brave to team up with my crazy friend, good ole Joe." Dmitri pointed to Joe.

"Oh, you flatter me too much." Joe tried to get up from the sidewalk. "Need some help here. My knees are locking up."

Dmitri and Joe chuckled as one helped the other to stand up on his feet.

"I have to show you the rental Harley," Joe said to Dmitri. "It has a Revolution Max 975T engine. A beauty, I tell you."

"Huh. At your age, you need four wheels instead of two."

And they laughed again.

The FBI On-Scene Commander arrived and greeted Dmitri, and then he explained the process to the group of four, the new A Team.

"Yes, you can make your statements at the hospital," he said. "Not all of these kids are yours, right?"

"No, only this one." Phoebe pointed to Jamie. Then she pointed to Hanley. "That's Maysie Madison-Greer's son, Hanley."

"I see."

"You know her?" Phoebe's eyebrows rose.

The OSC nodded.

"I told him everything Joe told me." Dmitri seemed so proud of himself. "Only problem was, it was late data, so they had to scramble. But at least they've arrived now."

"Thank you," Keenan said to the OSC.

Hanley, whom Keenan had carried out of the auction room, now refused to leave him. "I want to stay with your family, Uncle Keenan."

"Your mommy is looking for you," Joe said. "She is awake now in the hospital."

"Oh, is Maysie okay?" Phoebe asked.

"She's fine. Has a concussion," Joe said. "When I was waiting for you in the car, I talked to Kyle."

"In the middle of the night?" Keenan asked.

"Don't blame me. He called me when he couldn't get a hold of you or Phoebe."

"My phone is probably still at your house." Phoebe sighed.

From the corner of her eye, she saw that Esperanza was chatting with Dmitri.

"I'll take care of her," Dmitri said. "She's in bigger trouble than just child trafficking."

They must be talking about Noreen.

"We'll make sure she doesn't disturb your people ever again," Dmitri added.

"I owe you one," Esperanza said.

"I'll collect later." Dmitri pointed a finger at Joe. "Don't retire!"

Joe simply laughed.

Behind them, FBI agents had brought out many of the children and teenagers from the auction house. They were being carried or walked toward buses that had started to arrive.

Phoebe assumed that some of the agents in plainclothes had worked undercover at the nightclub, but she didn't recognize any of them. She made a mental note to be more observant in her next assignment.

Next assignment?

Right now all Phoebe wanted was to go home, take a shower, and go to bed.

"Where are they taking the kids?" Phoebe asked.

"They're all going to the hospital first, and we will be working to reunite them with their parents," the OSC said. "We'll take these three boys you rescued."

"Good." Phoebe wiped away tears of joy seeing the kids being escorted out. "They're going home to their families. Praise the Lord!"

And then she prayed that they had good families to return home to. Otherwise, the poor kids would suffer without succor.

"It's over now." Keenan hugged Phoebe and Jamie together.

"Mommy, I love you." Jamie kissed Phoebe on the cheek. Then he did the same for Keenan. "Daddy, I love you."

"We love you too," Phoebe said. "More than you'll ever know."

"I prayed that you would come get me," Jamie said.

"And we did, with God's help," Keenan said. "God answered your prayer, buddy."

"God is good," Jamie said.

"Amen," Phoebe and Keenan said in unison.

CHAPTER 11

Five weeks later...

The smell of sizzling ribeye rose into the August evening outside the O'Tierney cabin overlooking a glorious sunset across the Great Smoky Mountains.

Chatter and laughter of adults and children playing on the porch were music to Keenan's ears. All was well now in the household.

Surrounded by love, Jamie and his cousins from Savannah laughed and rolled around as they played with Hot Wheels and built castles. How those two things worked together was beyond Keenan, but it didn't matter.

Hanley was playing with the kids, but he was a quiet child, so Keenan didn't hear him talk. Maysie had dropped him off earlier without staying. She said that she couldn't leave Mrs. Madison alone at home, and the latter didn't want to sit in the car for twenty minutes to get here.

Every now and then, Keenan could hear peals of

laughter from Phoebe and Tamsyn as the two sisters listened to their father tell a joke. It wasn't even funny, from the sound of it, but it entertained the two women endlessly.

Tamsyn was married to architect Ryan Ruttledge, and they lived in an old Queen Anne house in Savannah, Georgia. Keenan and Phoebe had visited them the Christmas before.

This week, only Tamsyn and the kids flew out here with their grandparents. Ryan was in Atlanta finishing up a project for Midtown Chapel, a city church that a number of Christian employees at Mendenhall Security attended when they were in town.

"Tell another dad joke, Grandpa!" Alexi's voice echoed all the way to the grill.

"Please don't!" Jerome's wife, Rhoda, joked. "My stomach hurts!"

When Keenan met Phoebe seven years ago, Alexi had been seven years old and already adopted by Pastor Daniel Myers and his wife, Darlene. The otherwise childless couple had done a superb job raising the girl to be the polite and wonderful teenager that she was now. They even allowed her to visit Phoebe during school breaks so that Alexi would develop a relationship with her biological mother.

"You need any help, Chef Keenan?" Pastor Daniel's voice reached him.

Keenan turned to see the fifty-something man walk toward him. He was carrying a jug of lemonade.

"I'm fine. I could use a refill though." Keenan lifted up his empty glass.

"You're grilling for a lot of people." Pastor Daniel

filled the glass. "I don't mind helping, although I burn half the steaks I cook. What's your secret?"

"Trial and error." Keenan chuckled.

"Just like life. Thanks for the sermon tip. I'll preach about it next Sunday."

Keenan glanced at him. He sounded serious.

"My sermons come from real life experiences," Pastor Daniel explained.

"No wonder they resonate with me." Keenan didn't ask him why he was still an associate pastor at his church instead of the senior pastor.

Then again, he already knew why. The senior pastor was pushing eighty, but he was still going strong. Until the senior pastor retired or passed away, it was highly unlikely for junior pastors to preach regularly. They might fill in every now and then, but that was about it.

"Everyone likes their steaks done differently," Keenan said. "You can't please everyone."

"Yeah. What I tell them. There's always the microwave if the steak is too rare." Pastor Daniel put the lemonade jug down on the side table next to the grill. "I'll watch and learn."

"Okay." Keenan liked that about Pastor Daniel. He was always looking to learn something new. Even though he was a wealth of Bible truths and data, he was still open to learning new things in God's world.

"Thank you again for your counseling these weeks," Keenan said.

"God is good." Pastor Daniel pointed to the sky with his finger. "To God be the glory."

What a humble man.

Keenan was truly grateful to God for sending

Pastor Daniel their way. With his counseling, Keenan and Phoebe were better able to handle Jamie's recovery. Maysie and Hanley also received counseling from the pastor at no charge.

Even though Jamie and Hanley had only been abducted for a total of eleven hours—from the time they'd been taken at Mrs. Madison's house in Misty Mountain to the time they were rescued from the auction house in College Park, Georgia—it had been a harrowing experience for the four-year-olds.

By the mercy of God, the boys' trauma had been shortened because they had been the last ones to arrive at the auction house that evening.

Also, God provided an unexpected blessing to Jamie through his buddy, Hanley. They'd play LEGO blocks together and watch Scooby Doo on a small television with the other eight or nine kids about their age, all locked in the same room.

Whenever Jamie started to ask for his mommy, Hanley would distract him with toys. Whenever there were screams and fights outside their room, Hanley would tell him to focus on playing and watching TV.

How could a child that young have endured such things? Hanley's life with his father must've been a nightmare.

Keenan felt strongly that kids should be innocent and care free. School should be fun. Play should be easy. Life should be simple.

And yet the real world was often not so.

The smoke from the grill started to get into Keenan's eyes, assaulting his tear ducts. He blinked a couple of times.

Thank You, Jesus.

Keenan was overwhelmed by the mercy of God as he sipped a glass of lemonade while he flipped the steaks. "Mmm."

He looked forward to coming home to dinner every evening after work instead of eating takeout in a hotel or safe house somewhere. He'd rather eat home-cooked meals because then he knew what went in them. No bad chemicals or food dyes. He and Phoebe had determined to feed their family only natural foods.

Well, the time would come when Keenan could spend more time with his family. For now, Esperanza had decided to let them have two months off from work so that they could receive counseling and recover as a family.

Meanwhile, Joe decided to move his knee replacement surgery to the week after Phoebe returned to work in her new position as the deputy director of Mendenhall Retreat. That way, he could close out his illustrious career in military-related fields.

However, Joe had told Keenan that he wasn't ready to retire. After all, Dmitri had reminded him not to. In fact, Joe had started working on an investment project near Breckenridge B&B.

Keenan was sure that Joe would work and work until his dying day.

As for himself, Keenan hadn't thought of his future retirement yet. He was focused on the here and now. He wanted to provide for his wife and son, and wanted to save up enough so that they could travel and go on vacation if they wanted to.

For now, they were in their own house, but

Keenan was surprised by how happy Phoebe and Jamie were just to be at home with him. They didn't seem to want to be anywhere else. This was their place.

Keenan suspected that his time off would've been shorter if it wasn't for the fact that Esperanza and her corporate lawyers had to hammer out his new job description as the chief of security at the retreat.

It might seem unusual to some people that the retreat had no security department per se. However, Lamar and Esperanza had been the co-chiefs of the retreat that they owned. After Lamar was murdered, Esperanza continued to watch over the retreat while trying to branch out to Atlanta. Stretched too thin, she plodded on until now, when she found the right person to handle matters.

In the interim, Keenan often worried that he was missing something at Mendenhall Security. What juicy assignments had bypassed him because he was home resting? Why not allow him to sit in on the meetings? He could offer advice and such.

But no.

Esperanza, the big sister—or bossy aunt—that she positioned herself to be, had insisted that Keenan do nothing but spend time with his family for eight whole weeks. He had three more weeks to go before Esperanza let him have the new position.

Just as well because Keenan should start getting used to taking a backseat to all the action. At forty-three years old, his bones had begun to tell him that it was time to hang up the quarterback helmet for good and consider coaching as his next career move.

Already, Esperanza had hinted that she wasn't

going to let him retire into the position of chief of security at the retreat. He would be involved in training new members of Mendenhall Security while keeping residents and guests safe at the mountaintop hideaway.

His own lovely wife agreed that the job combination would keep him busy for years to come.

Keenan's biggest bonus of all was being able to watch his son grow up.

So far, he'd left all the child-rearing to Phoebe. Being a mother was a full-time job to begin with, but now she also had to work forty hours at the retreat.

It would be one of their greatest challenges of all to raise a child because the success of the training would be difficult to evaluate until the child had reached adult age. But without training, Proverbs 22:6 said the child might go astray.

> *Train up a child in the way he should go,*
> *And when he is old he will not depart from it.*

Keenan and Phoebe would need omniscient and omnipotent God every day to make it all work out.

"You made it!" Phoebe said aloud.

Keenan turned to see who it was.

Esperanza Diaz-Mendenhall with a Band-Aid on her forehead.

"What happened to you?" Phoebe stepped off the porch and was barefoot on the lawn that Keenan had mowed that morning.

Keenan left his grill and walked toward Esperanza.

"I'm okay. Just a small cut." Esperanza turned

toward the grill. "Mmm... Smells good. Too bad I can't stay."

"Not even for dinner? A girl's gotta eat," Phoebe pleaded.

Esperanza shook her head. "I'm here to tell you two something. Somewhere private we can talk?"

"My attic office." Keenan glanced back and saw Jerome walking toward the grill.

He waved to Keenan. "I got this, Son!"

Either Jerome had great hearing, or he had immediately assumed that Esperanza's presence meant work.

"Maybe ten minutes?" Keenan said to his father-in-law.

"Take your time," Jerome said. "I'll put the next batch of steaks on."

"Thank you." At this point in time, Keenan let his steaks go. He didn't worry about whether they'd turn out right for everyone. If Esperanza needed to talk privately, it was a bigger deal than maintaining his grilling reputation.

The trio navigated LEGO blocks on the porch on their way through the kitchen and hallway. Upstairs in Keenan's office, Phoebe closed the door behind them.

"Dmitri tracked Noreen to a private island in French Polynesia, and the FSB caught her." Esperanza sat down on a small couch. "She's on her way to Moscow as we speak."

Keenan had been informed that once Noreen was on Dmitri's radar, his counterparts at the Federal Security Service of the Russian Federation might get involved. Just as well, because nabbing Noreen had been outside the ability of Mendenhall Security, a private firm who didn't have the vast resources of the CIA or FSB.

"Dmitri is not FSB, though," Phoebe said.

"No. He's CIA, but when he handed Noreen over to his Russian friends, it was a favor that the FSB would probably repay in the future."

"Clever."

"Sometimes we have to remember that in the world we operate in, diplomacy can come in many forms, and is often an integral piece of the puzzle," Esperanza explained. "Even at Mendenhall Security, we try to use diplomacy first."

"Less bloodshed." Phoebe sat down next to Esperanza.

Every moment seemed to be a teaching moment for Esperanza. Keenan often wondered if he could level up to that point, where life lessons simply popped up everywhere every day.

Keenan chose to stand, leaning against his cluttered office desk.

"She was walking on a pier on her private island," Esperanza continued.

"Her?"

"Yeah, her customers paid her well. I can't tell you the name of the island, though." Esperanza leaned back. She looked tired—like she, too, needed to cut back on her working hours. "When the drones and choppers arrived, she tried to jump into the ocean. Can you believe it? How cowardly is that? A tropical storm was brewing, so she'd be lost forever."

"Intentionally, as in a suicide attempt?" Keenan asked.

"The FSB anticipated her desperation. Divers were ready. They fished her out immediately and saved her life."

Keenan waited for more. He knew Esperanza would tell them what she could. Perhaps this would end the blight on Keenan's career once and for all.

"They weren't going to let her escape trial by taking her own life, even though she might end up on death row anyway," Esperanza said.

"Why FSB? Why not MI5 or MI6?" Keenan asked.

"Turns out that while she was 'dead,' she got involved with some rebels bombing businesses in Moscow. The Russian government wanted her extradited to stand trial for the bombing of a theater in which several prominent Russian politicians and their families perished."

"Now she's a mass murderer?" Phoebe asked. "She has come a long way."

"Qatar also wants her for the murder of Omar's two wives and three kids. They offered the swift sword of a firing squad."

"They won't get her, right?" Phoebe asked.

Esperanza shook her head. "The FSB wants more information about their rebels, and they hope that Noreen might cut a deal to extend her life."

"Oh, I forgot to offer you something to drink." Phoebe gently tapped her own forehead. "I'll go downstairs to get you some. What would you like?"

"No need. I have to go." Esperanza got up from the couch and stretched. "No rest for the weary, as they say."

"Stay for a steak dinner?" Keenan asked.

"Sorry, I really can't. I have to fly out in an hour," Esperanza said. "I came home to get some clean clothes. I was going to call you from my cabin, but I decided to just drop in."

Keenan had learned not to ask Esperanza questions about where she was going or what she was doing.

Esperanza turned to Phoebe, who also got up from the couch. "I wanted to see you myself and make sure you're not distressed five weeks after the drama."

"By the grace of God, I'm fine," Phoebe answered. "If anything, I'm more prepared now for my job."

"Oh?"

"And I'm more prepared to protect my family." Keenan put his good arm over Phoebe's shoulder and gently squeezed it. "Both of us."

"Good." Esperanza pointed to Keenan. "You'll have plenty of opportunities to protect families as the chief of security for this retreat. Many of the recovering agents are bringing their families with them so that they can move forward together."

"Ready to help," Keenan said.

"It's been a long time coming." Esperanza sighed. "I don't know why Lamar and I never thought of hiring a chief of security."

"Back then, this retreat was relatively unknown, and you and Lamar handled everything," Phoebe suggested.

"I will always miss the big guy." Keenan couldn't help feeling nostalgic as he remembered his old friend, Lamar. They had been through a lot together and had saved each other's lives countless times.

Unfortunately, he had been unable to save

Lamar's life that very last time they'd both been held hostage.

Esperanza nodded. "It's hard, but we must press on."

The notion of pressing on reminded Keenan of Philippians 3:13-14, one of his favorite Bible verses.

Brethren, I do not count myself to have apprehended; but one thing I do, forgetting those things which are behind and reaching forward to those things which are ahead, I press toward the goal for the prize of the upward call of God in Christ Jesus.

Phoebe gave her boss a hug. "Thank you for caring."

"What are big sisters for?"

"Don't let Tamsyn hear it. She might think she has competition." Phoebe chuckled.

"Is she here tonight?"

Phoebe nodded. "She flew in this morning with her kids and my parents."

"Good to have family in town." Esperanza paused, as if trying to remember something. "Oh yeah. VenomLabs wants me to thank you for testing out the armored suits that night in Atlanta."

"Have they read my scathing report?" Keenan laughed.

"Every one of your reports is scathing. What else is new?" Esperanza chuckled.

"When will the testing end?" Phoebe asked.

Esperanza shrugged. "As long as they keep letting us test it, I'll keep asking for sponsorship of our missions."

"Clever."

"They want me to test it again on this mission. This time it will cost them quite a bit of money. I'm going home to Spain to see my grandparents, and I'm taking Leilani and Marie with me to show them our European operations."

"Marie is an old hat, but looks like Leilani is getting field training right away," Keenan said.

"Good for her. I didn't get to travel all eight years," Phoebe said.

"Don't wish for it, or it might come true." Esperanza wagged a finger.

"No, no. I want to stay home." Phoebe shook her hands side by side in front of her.

"I know. Each of the people I recruit has a different personality. I knew you'd rather stay at the retreat. Home is your happy place."

"You're so right, Espy," Phoebe said.

"On the other hand, Leilani spent a gap year hiking around the world with her friends before she finished college, and she speaks three Asian languages fluently. So let's see what comes of it."

"Between Marie and Leilani, you'll have the whole linguistic world covered," Keenan said.

"I try." Esperanza chuckled, then got serious. She pointed to the Band-Aid on her forehead. "You know how I got this?"

Neither Keenan nor Phoebe said a word because they knew Esperanza too well. It wasn't a question. It was a whole iceberg of a lesson coming up.

"If Taylor Solomon hadn't grabbed my collar, I'd be in a body bag of bones right now when the cable snapped sixty floors up." Esperanza's eyes watered.

Phoebe leaned over to hug her boss. "Thank God that you're still alive, Espy."

"I spun around and smashed my forehead on the cut glass, but Taylor had more stitches on his torso because he'd reached out through the broken window."

Keenan couldn't imagine what Esperanza would write in her report.

"I just feel that we've worked so well together," Esperanza said. "Since we're both owners of our own companies, I suggested a merger. That way we can share resources and multiply our profits."

"And it's always good to have a partner," Keenan added.

"But no. Taylor didn't want to go on working. He only has five people in his company, including himself and his administrator. He sold me his company."

"Just like that?" Phoebe asked. "Why didn't he just come work for you? He could always do a desk job and not have to go out in the field."

"He's burned out. He doesn't want to do anything anymore. He's now sitting at his ranch in Wyoming."

"Contemplating life?" Keenan asked.

"No, trying to sell that ranch and the forty thousand acres around it."

"Then what will he do? Does he have savings?"

"I didn't ask. That's kind of a personal question, you know," Esperanza said. "Then again, at our retreat, we're in the business of helping people recover and get back on their feet, so anything can happen. In fact, I invited him to come stay here awhile after he sells his Wyoming property."

"Maybe he could do some part-time work for us."

Keenan couldn't begin to list Taylor's skills. They had been all and sundry.

"He has to sort out his life first," Esperanza said. "He's still not talking to his dad after his dad sold Solomon Security to someone else. It seems that their rift will never be mended, especially since his own brand of Taylor Solomon has fallen flat."

"Yeah, Taylor has a very specialized skillset, but he's not as business savvy as his dad."

"That's the truth. Security companies need funding and clients, and Taylor can get neither." Without being prompted, Esperanza said more. "I want to be there for him."

Perhaps something else was brewing between Esperanza and her loyal friend from Vancouver. He had always been there for her ever since Lamar passed away. Never too close, but he'd answer Esperanza at the first phone ring.

"To whom did his dad sell Solomon Security?" Phoebe asked the more important question.

"Benjamin Glynn."

Billionaire treasure hunter Benjamin Glynn was yet another friend of Esperanza's. As far as Keenan knew, she had been trying to invite Benjamin to invest in Mendenhall Security for years.

Instead of doing so, he'd bought his own security team. He fired half of the personnel, and turned the team into a private one that protected only him and his family's vested interests.

If Benjamin needed more help, then he'd call Esperanza, whose Mendenhall Security was for hire 24/7.

"Interesting that you're friends with both Taylor,

the one who didn't inherit his father's business, and Benjamin, who owns Taylor's family business," Phoebe said.

"Life is funny sometimes." Esperanza shrugged. "So there we were—Taylor and me—in the hospital, and I didn't want to leave him alone after he'd sold me his company. So I asked him to imagine with me a future in which we worked together."

"Because you wanted him to rise from the ashes." Phoebe's eyes glistened. "You're always saving abandoned puppies and orphaned cats, Espy."

After Phoebe and Esperanza hugged, the latter continued her story.

"Anyway, we were dreaming of a new merger, which is a good time for me to update the name of the company. Neither of us liked hyphenated company names. Mendenhall-Solomon has too many syllables, for example."

Keenan didn't want to remind Esperanza that her own married last name was also hyphenated: Diaz-Mendenhall.

"What name did you come up with, Espy?" Phoebe asked.

"I've been thinking of Watchman Security, but in this age, we might get sued because we didn't say *Watchwoman* or *Watchperson*," Esperanza explained. "But I thought of it because of the watchman in Ezekiel 33:7."

Which Keenan happened to know by heart, so he recited it for all to hear.

So you, son of man: I have made you a watchman

for the house of Israel; therefore you shall hear a word from My mouth and warn them for Me.

"Taylor liked the concept, but he suggested we call the final company Watchfire instead of Watchman and keep Ezekiel 33:7 as our foundational verse. Win-win." Esperanza smiled, perhaps at a memory she wasn't sharing with her employees. "So now we just need to wait for another acquisition."

"How big is the company going to be?" Phoebe asked.

"Probably never too big due to Mendenhall Security's frequent turnovers," Keenan said. "The work is brutal and always dangerous, so people quit often."

"Mendenhall Security is aging. Most of us are in our forties. Some in their fifties," Esperanza said. "We need more juniors to join the ranks and train with us to keep the watchfire burning long after we're gone."

"Watchfire." Keenan warmed up to the name even though he wasn't working at Mendenhall Security anymore.

"Taylor will come in as a consultant. He and I will train the recruits, and so will you too." Esperanza pointed at Keenan. "Don't forget. You're not totally retiring into the retreat."

"Right." Keenan nodded.

"Taylor is a strong Christian, so we're of equal yoke, no?" Esperanza laughed.

Jokes aside, Keenan felt bad that they would eventually lose the name Mendenhall Security as the company expands. Then again, it wasn't like they—especially Esperanza—had forgotten Lamar Mendenhall. Mendenhall Retreat still bore his legacy.

Besides, Lamar hadn't started Mendenhall Security. Esperanza had been the one who'd poured all that she and Lamar had experienced into the company.

"I still remember the days when we didn't have a name," Keenan said. "It was just Lamar, you, me, and whoever else we could collaborate with—like Raj Subramaniam."

"Who used to be known as Roger six years ago?" Phoebe asked.

Esperanza nodded. "You might have met him when he stayed at the lodge whenever he wasn't at his Wyoming ranch."

"Raj should've stayed stateside every time, but he likes to see what's going on out there. He and that Logan guy, they both like to be involved." Esperanza wrinkled her nose. "It makes for all sorts of trouble as I have to find bodyguards for both of them."

Logan Urquhart and Raj were both major clients of Mendenhall Security. Neither of them knew how to handle weapons in the field, but they were both billionaires with a wealth of knowledge in managing successful ventures. Esperanza picked their business brains, and they hired her company to keep their people safe.

"Logan's got his own wife to keep him safe," Keenan remarked.

"But Marie's job is almost always at the Atlanta office," Esperanza said. "She can translate and analyze remotely. She has zero travel requirements."

"Between Raj and Logan, you have your hands full." Phoebe sounded like she felt sorry for Esperanza's people problems.

Esperanza glanced at her phone. "I have to go."

"Since you're here but you can't stay, how about I make you a to-go dinner box?" Phoebe asked.

"Oh, I'd like that. Beats eating hamburgers on the flight."

"For sure. Nothing can beat a steak dinner. Keenan's steaks are the best."

Keenan cleared his throat. "Well, Jerome has taken over the grill."

"Then it's a hit or miss." Phoebe walked toward the office door. "Do you have five minutes? I can pack up a meal for you."

Esperanza glanced at her watch. "They're not going to leave without me, so yes, I can spare five minutes."

Phoebe left the office and ran downstairs. Keenan's prosthetics climbed down the stairs more slowly than his wife. He let Esperanza go first.

"How long are you going to be gone this time?" Keenan asked. He held on to the railing. He didn't want to tumble down onto Esperanza and smash her with his prosthetics.

"A few months. Maybe more, but no less."

"That long?"

"Since you two are running the retreat as soon as your sabbaticals are over, I can leave for longer periods of time."

"Oh, has that been the plot the entire time?" Keenan chuckled.

"Here's the thing. I'm in my forties now, and I don't know how long I can jump around. My quarter-back days are coming to a close."

Somehow, Keenan doubted it. Esperanza was the

fittest woman he knew. It would shock him if she retired anytime soon. She was only forty-five years old.

"Maybe you need longer down-time in between missions," Keenan said.

"I second that!" Phoebe was at the foot of the stairs, holding a clear plastic bag that contained a paper dinner box. There were even napkins and a plastic fork and knife on top of the box.

Either Keenan had been coming down the stairs slowly or Phoebe had been fast as lightning, packing dinner for Esperanza.

"Your dinner, ma'am, in less than five minutes." Phoebe lifted the plastic bag in the air. "You can reheat the dinner box in the airplane."

"Am I being pampered before I'm the boss?" Esperanza reached the bottom of the stairs and took the free dinner from Phoebe.

"You're the queen of Mendenhall Retreat," Phoebe said. "When you come home, we'll pamper you at this inclusive and exclusive retreat."

"Now go and get them," Keenan said. "Just don't do anything I wouldn't do."

"I'm the one who has to rein both of you in." Esperanza laughed.

And laughed all the way out the front door to her car.

EPILOGUE

Five months later...

Nestled on top of the Great Smoky Mountains, Mendenhall Retreat was isolated, with only one road in and out of it and a helipad for VIP guests.

A hideaway for clandestine operatives, Mendenhall Retreat usually operated at ninety percent capacity. The remaining ten percent occupancy was usually filled in no time, with a waiting list that could be weeks or months long.

At the heart of the retreat, the Mendenhall Lodge was a sprawling building surrounded by gardens, walking trails, outdoor gathering spaces, and an array of log cabins of all sizes around it.

Working at Mendenhall Retreat had its perks, including free breakfast and lunch, two meals that Phoebe tried not to miss. Even if she wasn't all that hungry, she'd try to eat a salad or something light.

Today, her appetite had returned, and Phoebe devoured a feast at lunch. She had soup and salad, plus baby back ribs—slathered with Carolina sauce—and two servings of apple pie.

She could barely waddle back to her office on the other side of the lodge. Along the way, she walked by a wall of large windows overlooking the mountain ranges, where brown leafless trees interspersed with evergreens stretching as far as her eyes could see.

Up in the sky, dark clouds hovered over the Mendenhall Retreat. Phoebe suspected it would sleet or snow.

She stared into the distance, when someone came up behind her and wrapped familiar arms around her waist.

"Hey, sweetheart. Whatcha thinking about?" Keenan whispered in her ear.

"I was wondering if it might snow again." Phoebe leaned back against her husband's chest. His old barn jacket, almost threadbare, was warm.

"Maybe. The weather forecast said it's not going to rise above thirty-one degrees today. It'll stay this way over the weekend." Keenan pointed. "There. Snowing now."

Phoebe peered. She could see nothing...

Oh, she saw it now.

"Just some snow flurries. Will they stick?"

"Maybe. After all, January is the time for snow." He nuzzled her neck. "Maybe we should take a walk in the woods tomorrow after we sleep in."

"It feels like this week just zipped by. It was just Saturday, wasn't it? And now it will be Saturday again in less than twelve hours."

In a way, Phoebe was glad it was Friday. Since they had rescued Jamie back in July, she had worked non-stop in her new position as the deputy director. The first few weeks were spent shadowing the outgoing deputy director, Joe Brannigan.

Joe had been happy to retire, but he hadn't gone quietly. He had somehow managed to persuade Dad and Rhoda to move to the new senior living community two blocks away from Breckenridge B&B. The Breckenridge family had purchased the bankrupted extended stay hotel and turned it into the Misty Mountain Senior Living community with floors for both independent and assisted living.

Phoebe thought that the MMSL had been a strategic move. With one purchase, the Breckenridges got rid of the chain hotel competing with their business on the same street, and at the same time provided a badly needed service to the community whose population included the aging, such as Mrs. Madison.

Speaking of her, Mrs. Madison also moved into the MMSL. That freed up Maysie to find a full-time job outside of the house.

Newell Greer was in jail in Gatlinburg after having been convicted of child trafficking and violence against Maysie. Even though Newell had committed the crime in Misty Mountain, the small town only had a small prison. Gatlinburg agreed to house him at their state-of-the-art penitentiary.

His ex-girlfriend also testified against him, and received a reduced jail time in return.

After the trial ended and she had recovered from her injuries, Maysie Madison-Greer left town with Hanley. She wanted to find a place where her ex-husband wouldn't think of looking for them.

Mrs. Madison sent Phoebe updates whether she

wanted to hear them or not. In any case, while they were keeping warm in snowy Misty Mountain, Maysie was driving around sunny Texas in her camper van.

She homeschooled Hanley, but as soon as they settled down somewhere, she'd transfer him to a regular school. If she wasn't a single mother, she would have stayed home to care for Hanley. However, times were tough and money was tight, so Maysie was doing the best she could.

Mrs. Madison had gone on and on about the rest of it, but Phoebe couldn't remember the details now. She'd been busy with her work and making sure that Jamie wouldn't be abducted again.

She felt less burden about that because Keenan had left his job at Mendenhall Security, and was now the chief of security at Mendenhall Retreat. It was almost a low pressure job for him, considering the type of work he used to do for Esperanza when he had to fly all over the world.

On the other hand, as the retreat's security chief, Keenan worked nine to five at the lodge, five minutes from their cabin, oversaw five other security personnel and a dozen drones, and never had to travel out of town.

Therefore, their family of three had been enjoying dinner together every night for the last several months. Phoebe felt that their family was closer now more than ever. Every now and then, Alexi and her adopted parents would come over to visit, now that Phoebe was too busy to take Jamie to see his half sister.

The Myers had just spent Christmas week at the

O'Tierney home. There were only two bedrooms in their small cabin, so the two siblings slept in sleeping bags in front of the fireplace in the living room.

Phoebe had taken the opportunity to ask Alexi's adopted father whether he'd consider becoming the Mendenhall Retreat chaplain and senior pastor at the Mendenhall Chapel.

It wasn't too clear whether being a senior pastor at the smaller Mendenhall Chapel, with its transient congregation, might be less stressful than being an associate pastor at his old Mountain Chapel.

However, it turned out that Pastor Daniel had been ready for a change. He'd been an associate pastor at his old church for thirty years, never leveling up because they could only have one senior pastor.

Besides, his wife, Darlene, who had worked for many years in their church's preschool department, would love to run the Mendenhall Daycare. She also thought that it would be a good thing for Alexi, their only child, to spend more time with her half-brother, Jamie.

After Esperanza's husband, Lamar, had been murdered some years ago in a cabin near Phoebe's, Esperanza turned that cabin into a chapel in memory of Lamar. Visiting pastors came and went, but Phoebe had persuaded Esperanza to hire a permanent pastor for the small church. This pastor would also minister to the residents and guests who came through the retreat each year.

To his credit, Pastor Daniel said that he and his wife, Darlene, would pray about it and get back to Phoebe by the spring. It was a positive conversation. Phoebe thought they were leaning toward saying yes because it would bring Alexi and Jamie closer as siblings. They were the only children in their own homes otherwise. Since they were a homeschooling family, they could move anywhere at any time. The entire world was their classroom, as the saying went.

Keenan released his arms around Phoebe. "Better let you get back to work."

"But we've both been here since seven o'clock, so if we stay until five, that's ten hours."

"With a two-hour lunch break?" Keenan chuckled.

"Not really." Phoebe checked her phone. "Barely an hour."

"It's a good thing that the after-school care is now operational. Otherwise, I wouldn't feel good about leaving Jamie in someone else's care for nine or ten hours each day."

Operational?

Phoebe smiled at her husband's choice of words. He still thought like someone in the special forces, even though he'd left that profession years ago. However, Keenan wasn't fully retired from that type of career. Every now and then, Esperanza might still call for his help for certain missions, and he'd go.

As for Phoebe, she would stay home and run the retreat and keep an eye on their only son. If not for the after-school facility in a small cabin in the back-yard of the lodge, Phoebe might not have even taken the deputy director job at all.

Not that she was hovering over Jamie. God had protected Jamie and returned him to her, so she wanted to be the best mom she could be for him. That included being present in his life and always being there whenever he needed her.

Would she like to have more kids? Sure. If the Lord blessed them, it would be a good thing for Jamie to have another sibling closer to his age. Alexi was ten years older and a teenager now.

"I'll walk you back to your office on my way to the range," Keenan said.

"Okay." Phoebe didn't remind him that it would be a detour for him to go to her office first because the elevator to the gun range in the basement was at another part of the lodge.

"What do you want to do tomorrow?" Keenan walked with Phoebe down the hallway, nodding to guests who passed by them. "I don't mean to make us all go walk in the woods."

"I don't feel the pressure," Phoebe said. "You and Jamie could go play in the snow. I'll stay home in my pajamas and read a book."

Saturdays were their stay-at-home days. Sundays, they went to church, and then sometimes ate out and visited friends after church.

Phoebe enjoyed the routine because everything was predictable. No surprises, no drama.

Even the people who came to stay at Mendenhall Retreat had come to rest from their world of worries, so they wouldn't be the ones to stir up trouble for anyone else staying there.

By the time they arrived at the check-in counter, they were often exhausted from projects that had taken every ounce of their energy. The retreat offered a soft bed, hot meals, and a private space to rejuvenate and recalibrate.

With the addition of Mendenhall Chapel, guests' spiritual needs could be met as well. Most of the time, they didn't bring families with them, but the onsite daycare could open the doors to healing for couples. If their kids were taken care of, then they could spend time dealing with recovery and whatever ailed them.

Mendenhall Retreat was shaping up nicely. Under Phoebe and Keenan, guests felt safe and secure. Their needs were met, like getting a cup of cold water in a dry and thirsty land. Or food when their stomachs were hungry.

The blessings of a safe place and a great job all came from God. Phoebe's heart warmed as she felt gratefulness for all that God had done for her family. Truly, James 1:17 had been in action. That was the verse that Phoebe and Keenan had read shortly after she became pregnant, and the reason they'd named their son James.

Every good gift and every perfect gift is from above, and comes down from the Father of lights, with whom there is no variation or shadow of turning.

Next thing Phoebe knew, they had reached her office door. Keenan hadn't said anything to her since they started walking from the windows.

"Sorry. I didn't mean to ignore you." Phoebe kissed her husband on his cheek. "My mind was somewhere else. Among other things, I was thinking about the goodness of God in James 1:17."

"God is good indeed. We have gone through fire and flood, and He has delivered us through them all." Keenan held Phoebe's hands.

"Will you come get me at five when you finish work?" Phoebe unlocked her office door.

"I'll go pick up Jamie first, and we'll both come get you."

"Sounds good. See you then."

No sooner had Phoebe put her work phone down on her table, it buzzed. A text message arrived from Marie Bouchard at the Mendenhall Security office in Atlanta. Phoebe noticed that she had messaged both Phoebe and Keenan using the highest encryption on their company-issued phones.

MARIE

Espy and her team are injured.

PHOEBE

Oh no!

MARIE

Please prepare three rooms at the lodge, and one cabin that can accommodate six people. And ask housekeeping to air out Espy's cabin.

PHOEBE

Got it. ETA?

MARIE

Tonight. Who's the doctor on call?

PHOEBE

Two, actually. Selma and Truitt.

MARIE

Good. Thanks.

Silently, Phoebe asked God to protect Esperanza, who had been like the most caring older sister to her. Of course, Phoebe also had an adopted sister back in

Savannah, Georgia, with whom she'd spent eighteen years of her younger life.

However, Esperanza had been there in Phoebe's adult years until now. In many ways, Phoebe owed her and didn't want to see her hurt in any way.

Phoebe couldn't recall the last time Esperanza was hurt. This current mission of hers was in Atlanta, so couldn't she just stay there? The big metropolis had hospitals and hotels. Besides, Esperanza also owned a house near her Atlanta office.

MARIE

Keenan, you there?

KEENAN

Yes. Listening.

MARIE

FPCON Delta.

KEENAN

Got it.

MARIE

Thanks, you two.

PHOEBE

Stay safe. I'm praying.

Force Protection Condition Delta was the highest threat level for Mendenhall Retreat. The last time the retreat's security level elevated to FPCON Delta, the Vice President of the United States recuperated here after a surgery that had nearly taken his life.

Could it be him again this time? If so, the couple whom Marie had mentioned was probably the VP and his wife of forty years.

A knock on the door derailed Phoebe's thoughts. She looked up. "Oh, it's you again."

Keenan grinned. "I got the message too."

"Good. Now go back to work. Call me on the phone if you need anything."

He made a face. "I'm in your office precisely about work."

"Oh?"

Keenan closed the door behind him and walked toward her desk. He kept his voice low. "Never a dull moment, is there?"

"Next time, please remind me not to be too happy about the lack of drama at the retreat these days."

"Now it's different." Keenan was trying to get close to his wife.

"Discipline, Mr. O'Tierney." Phoebe motioned for him to take a seat on the other side of her desk.

"Why?" Keenan wrinkled his nose at her.

"Because it's two o'clock in the middle of a working afternoon, and I know you were about to come here to hug me."

"How did you guess?"

"We've been married for six-plus years." Phoebe laughed. "If you keep crossing the line at work, I'll ask Espy to send you back to Mendenhall Security."

"Espy doesn't need me there. She wants to recruit your stepbrother to work from the Atlanta office, as well as Jessica to fly planes for her." Keenan laughed and plopped down in his designated chair.

"She's always recruiting. Poor Garrett. I feel sorry for him." Phoebe paused. "Then again, when his contract is up in a year, he might want to work for Mendenhall Security when he's not a Reserve."

"His pay will double due to his special skillset, or even triple or quadruple it if Espy wants Garrett enough."

"That's how she works." Phoebe agreed with her husband. "I'd say that her motto is *carpe diem*, no matter the cost."

Seize the day.

Speaking of time, Phoebe almost forgot to do her job. She logged into her desktop computer. "I need to find three rooms at the lodge and one cabin to accommodate half a dozen people."

"Plus get housekeeping to air out Espy's cottage."

"That too." Phoebe jotted it down on a sticky note.

Since she had worked at the registration front desk before, that had become a useful skill now, even though she hardly ever checked guests in anymore as the deputy director. Esperanza had hired someone else to do the job.

"That was easy. We don't have full occupancy in January because the road up the mountain is usually iced over and treacherous." Phoebe double-checked her screen to make sure she had saved the reservations.

"Although maintenance often salts the road," Keenan reminded her.

"Right." Phoebe logged into the housekeeping system to request cabin cleaning. For good measure, she called the head of the housekeeping staff to double make sure she knew that Phoebe had logged in the request.

After she put down the phone, she turned to

Keenan. "Seriously, FPCON Delta. Are you thinking what I'm thinking?"

Keenan nodded. "The VP or his family has been threatened again."

"Espy is a close friend of SOTUS." Phoebe recalled how Esperanza had agonized over a Christmas present for the Second Lady of the United States. Phoebe had helped her select a brooch security camera that SOTUS wore almost all the time on her coat lapel.

"Which begs the question, what was Espy's current project that got her injured?" Keenan looked far away.

"You miss the action adventure?" Phoebe asked.

"That's all behind me. I'm actually very settled down and happy to be running security here at the retreat. I like this workload, it's easier on my prosthetics, and I get to see you and our son every day."

"I'm glad you're happy. I do like my job very much. I wouldn't have liked it eight years ago, but I'm older now, and I think Espy has trained me long enough to handle it. I learned so much shadowing her all these years."

"God has provided for us, as He always does." Keenan got up from his chair. "I'm heading to a meeting with my security team."

"You don't seem worried about FPCON Delta."

Keenan shook his head. "We've prepared for it, trained and rehearsed for it—on those slow days with nothing else to do. With God's help, I'll make sure we're all safe. After all, two of my most precious people are here, and it's my job to protect you and Jamie."

Phoebe couldn't help but feel content. A protector all the way through, Keenan guarded his loved ones with tenacity. Phoebe felt safe with Keenan here.

"I thank God for you." Phoebe got out of her chair and came around the desk to where Keenan sat.

Keenan held her hands gently as they smiled at each other. "I thank God for you too, Phoebe. Always."

And then they went back to work.

DEAR READER,

I hope you've enjoyed *Going Once, Going Twice*, a Christian suspense novel in my Guardian Sweethearts series of books that take place in between other series in my story world. The events in *Going Once, Going Twice* happened after *Reach for Me* (Vacation Sweethearts Book 2) and before *Once a Spy* (Protector Sweethearts Book 3).

The next book in there series after *Going Once, Going Twice* is *Fool Me Once, Fool Me Twice* (Guardian Sweethearts Book 4). In this story, Marie Bouchard, who made a cameo appearance in *Going Once, Going Twice*, will be featured along with her husband, billionaire Logan Urquhart. Sign up for my newsletter to be notified then *Fool Me Once, Fool Me Twice* is published.

Fool Me Once, Fool Me Twice
Guardian Sweethearts Book 4

JanThompson.com/fool

To be notified when this novel is published, sign up
for my book news mailing list:
JanThompson.com/newsletter

If you're new to my Guardian Sweethearts series,
it kicks off with *Once Bitten, Twice Shy* (Guardian
Sweethearts Book 1) that tells the story of private
investigator Ming Wei and his real estate agent wife,
Sabine, from *Tell You Soon* (Savannah Sweethearts
Book 3) as they investigate a cold case involving the
murder of Sabine's father. This novel takes place just
before *Once a Thief* (Protector Sweethearts Book 1).

Once Bitten, Twice Shy
Guardian Sweethearts Book 1
JanThompson.com/bitten

Going Once, Going Twice began six years after
Reach for Me ended. In *Reach for Me*, a Christian
romance novel with a side of suspense, Phoebe met
Keenan at the mountaintop Mendenhall Retreat
while both were in the valleys of their lives. Read this
novel to find out how they met and fell in love.

Reach for Me
Vacation Sweethearts Book 2
JanThompson.com/reach

If the names Marie and Logan are familiar to you,
you might recall their second-chance love story in
Wait for Me (Vacation Sweethearts Book 3).

Wait for Me
Vacation Sweethearts Book 3
JanThompson.com/wait

In *Reach for Me*, Phoebe's family members also appeared. Phoebe's sister, Tamsyn and their father, Jerome, appeared in *Walk You There* (Savannah Sweethearts Book 6), a Christian coastal romance set in the old colonial city of Savannah, Georgia. Tamsyn and Jerome were in attendance at the family reunion in *Going Once, Going Twice*.

Walk You There
Savannah Sweethearts Book 6
JanThompson.com/walk

Back to *Going Once, Going Twice*, to help with the near-impossible search for their missing child, Phoebe and Keenan must rely on technology. Two companies were involved in this novel.

Binary Systems, Inc., is based out of Atlanta. The two co-founders of the company, Cayson Yang and his cousin, Leland, are good friends of Esperanza Diaz-Mendenhall, who owns both Mendenhall Retreat and Mendenhall Security. Cayson's own story is told in *Zero Sum* (Binary Hackers Book 1).

Zero Sum
Binary Hackers Book 1
JanThompson.com/sum

Another Binary Systems hacker mentioned in *Going Once, Going Twice* is Iseul Kim, who helped

Phoebe and Joe to track down the child abductor. Iseul has her own problems to solve in *Zero Out* (Binary Hackers Book 3) when she tries to rescue her own brother trapped in the Himalayan mountains.

Zero Out
Binary Hackers Book 3
JanThompson.com/out

The second computer company involved in the search and rescue operation in *Going Once, Going Twice* is a smaller outfit called Still Salvage, based out of Still Waters community in North Georgia. The two young hackers, Havilah and Asher, make cameo appearances one year later in *Zero Trust* (Binary Hackers Book 4) along with Dmitri Proskouriakoff.

I mentioned that Keenan's prosthetics were experimental robotic devices made by VenomLabs. Another person who used a more advanced version of these prosthetics, including a bionic eye, is Dmitri's daughter, Mira, in the above-mentioned *Zero Trust*. In this novel, a wannabe vigilante hires a former soldier to track down and kill her mother's assassin, but... Well, if you're curious about this Christian romantic technothriller, check it out.

Zero Trust
Binary Hackers Book 4
JanThompson.com/trust

Going Once, Going Twice is the prelude to several upcoming novels. Stories featuring Esperanza Diaz-Mendenhall, Kyle Stewart, and Garrett Untermeyer are all coming soon. To be the first to know when their books are ready, please sign up for my book news mailing list.

Jan's Book News Mailing List
JanThompson.com/newsletter

Continue reading for a sneak peek of *Once Bitten, Twice Shy.*

READ THE FIRST NOVEL IN THE SERIES
GUARDIAN SWEETHEARTS BOOK 1

A cold case binds an estranged couple together.

While trying to fix their marriage, private investigator Ming Wei and his real estate agent wife, Sabine, investigate the unsolved murder of Sabine's father.

SABINE IS ON A MISSION...

Four years after their wedding, cracks appear in their marriage. Ming leaves for a multi-month project overseas, leaving his wife at home with two young kids and a business to run. To take her mind off their marital woes, Sabine helps her mother investigate her father's murder.

The undercover operation takes her through a shooting competition, which Sabine wins. Participants are invited to a mountain retreat where a banquet is to be held in their honor. Ever inching closer to danger, Sabine only has her sister, Helen, as backup.

MING RUSHES TO HER SIDE...

In spite of their personal problems, Ming can't live with himself for "abandoning" his wife and kids. He hands over the project to someone else and flies home only to find his mother-in-law babysitting their kids and dog, while his wife has gone to do something dangerous.

Ming gets involved and goes undercover to provide support for Sabine. The trail leads Sabine to people in the past, including her ex-boyfriend. Ming worries she might rekindle that old relationship. Against this backdrop, can Ming remain objective?

TROPES/THEMES:

• Alpha Hero
  • Asian Hero

- Strong Woman
- Smart Heroine
- Independent Woman
- Estranged Married Couple
- Asian American Romance
- Private Investigators
- Forced Proximity
- Cold Case
- Investigating an Old Murder

Once Bitten, Twice Shy is a married life Christian romantic suspense novel in between Tell You Soon (Savannah Sweethearts Book 3) and Once a Thief (Protector Sweethearts Book 1). The epilogue of *Once Bitten, Twice Shy* leads straight into Chapter One of Once a Thief.

In Tell You Soon, Ming and Sabine fell in love and married each other. In *Once Bitten, Twice Shy*, they now have two kids but their marriage is on the rocks. Somewhat separated, Ming works overseas while Sabine stays in Savannah to help Mom investigate Dad's death. If you recall, in Tell You Soon, Sabine mentioned that her father died in a mysterious road accident that was unsolved.

In her sister's story, Once a Thief, Helen and her mom (aka Mama Hu) commiserated about missing Dad. Well, in between those two books, we have *Once Bitten, Twice Shy*, in which we find out what happened to Edgar Hu, the founder of Hu Knows, Inc., investigative firm based in Savannah, Georgia, with worldwide clients.

ONCE BITTEN, TWICE SHY
SNEAK PEEK
PROLOGUE

After breaking his five-million-dollar work contract in Dubai, private investigator Ming Wei flew home to the States to apologize to his wife. In the cramped economy class, he had rehearsed everything he wanted to say to her as soon as he saw her.

At the Savannah/Hilton Head International Airport, he rented a car and drove himself home to Tybee Island. He still had the house keys.

He walked through the front door to find it all quiet. No one greeted him, not even Pickles, their senior golden retriever.

That was when he knew something was wrong.

The dog bowls—one for water and one for dry food—were gone. The dog's favorite treats were also gone.

Ming wandered around the house, hoping to hear Sabine's voice somewhere, laughing with their daughter, Hannah.

The entire house was bathed in silence.

In the master bathroom, Sabine's toothbrush and makeup were all gone. The closet still had clothes, but Sabine's favorite suitcase wasn't there.

The kids' rooms looked about the same.

He texted Sabine. No reply.

He called her. No answer.

He called his mother-in-law, Mama Hu. She picked up on the fourth ring. "Are Sabine and the kids at your house?"

"Well..."

"Tell me as it is. No need to try not to hurt my feelings. Where is Sabine?"

Mama Hu was silent.

"If she's in danger, your lack of response is going to be bad news." Ming was losing his cool.

"I don't like the way you talk to me. I'm going to hang up—"

"No, no. Please don't. I'm just worried about Sabine." Ming tried to calm down.

"I am too. But you don't have to be rude to me."

Something was up. Mama Hu sounded guilty.

"Mama Hu, don't you want Sabine and me to get

back together?" Ming blurted. He felt frustrated. Defeated, even.

"That's your fault, isn't it?"

At least Mama Hu had continued talking. Ming had to keep her going until she told him what he wanted to know.

"Don't let the sun go down on your anger," Mama Hu added.

She had clearly echoed Ephesians 4:26-27.

"Be angry, and do not sin": do not let the sun go down on your wrath, nor give place to the devil.

Even though Mama Hu wasn't a Christian, she knew a Bible verse or two. Perhaps it was due to the influence of her two daughters—one of whom was supposed to be the love of Ming's life.

"I'm sorry. It's my fault for not taking better care of Sabine and our kids." Ming had no choice. At least, that had been what he'd been telling himself for months, trying to keep his company out of bankruptcy. He still believed that he could keep Savannah River Investigations, Inc., afloat.

"Sabine is raising the children alone. You weren't there at Hannah's preschool event in December. You weren't even home for Thanksgiving, Christmas, or New Year's Day. What kind of a husband and father are you? Do your kids even remember what you look like?"

"I was only gone for three months."

"That's at least ninety days. Do you want me to count the hours?"

"I had to work."

"You could've worked in Georgia. Why Dubai? You love money more than your wife and kids."

There it was, the indictment.

Ming hung his head in shame. "I missed out on a lot. Gotta put food on the table."

"Food on the table with empty seats?" Mama Hu snarled. "You know Sabine. She doesn't care if you don't earn millions of dollars. She wants you there at family dinners. You're always MIA, even when you were working in the States. Now that you've started to take international clients, you're overseas a lot."

"After I get my business back on track, I'll do better."

"It might be too late, Ming. You missed all the important holidays and birthdays. You messed up, Ming."

Ming had to agree. "It's over now, and I'm home again."

"Was it worth it? Did you need the job so badly that you sacrificed your wife?"

"I'm not sacrificing Sabine." Not to mention he also lost the contract when he told his client in Dubai that he couldn't possibly have an affair with her.

Sigh.

Sabine had been right. Lorna—was that even her real name?—hadn't hired him just to investigate her fiancé's infidelity, but also to make him her lover, a little known fact Ming hadn't been aware of until just days ago, after almost three months of being in close proximity with her. He had considered it business, but apparently Lorna had a different idea.

"You left your wife alone for three months,"

Mama Hu repeated. "I'd be surprised if it was worth it."

"I had to take whatever job I could find to pay my bills. I'm deep in debt." Ming didn't want to talk about the albatross around his neck, but he was a hundred and sixty-seven thousand dollars in the red, due to the second mortgage he'd taken out on his office downtown plus advertising costs.

If things didn't turn around, he'd have to sell his office space and move his workspace into the toolshed in his backyard. His original home office upstairs had been converted into Hannah's playroom. Maybe he could reclaim it.

Sabine had offered to invest in SRI, but Ming had refused it. He wanted them to use her savings to pay for the children's school. He did not want Sabine to take her inheritance from her dad plus the money she'd earned from selling her shares of Hu Knows just to pay off his company debt. If things came to that, he would have to offer Sabine a share of SRI.

Now he missed Sabine so much that he was willing to do anything to get his family back. He might even sell SRI to another private investigator, if there was someone out there willing to take over his loan payments.

Money management was something that he wasn't good at. He recalled a long time ago in his bachelor days when he had to sell his beach house. Sabine had been his real estate agent. It was a good thing that his sister, Heidi, and her husband, Diego, had bought the house. At least it wasn't now a rental property for summer visitors.

"I don't care," Mama Hu snapped. "You left my

daughter to parent two kids alone. Your marriage is over."

Ming felt uncomfortable hearing what Mama Hu said. "As long as we're still married, there's still a chance..."

"She's already talking to a divorce lawyer."

Ming knew that through Helen, but he still felt that it wasn't over yet. "Our marriage vows said 'until death do us part.' I'm still alive."

"Oh no. Don't say death. Please don't say death." Mama Hu's voice shook.

"Mama Hu?"

"Yes?"

"Where exactly is Sabine?" Ming's heart was racing a mile a minute, but he kept his voice calm.

"She's not here. Only the kids and your dog that sheds everywhere are here."

"When's Sabine coming back?"

"Uh... I don't know. It depends on whether she could find her dad's pocket watch."

"Her what?" Ming tried to process what Mama Hu was saying. Before Edgar died, he had given his entire family pocket watches. They were made of gold, but they all had homing beacons and trackers in them. This had been back in the days before GPS was ubiquitous.

As far as Ming knew, Sabine kept hers in a safe at home. She never used it because it was the last gift from her father, and she already had GPS on her own phone. She said that Helen sometimes carried her pocket watch in her purse as a reminder of Dad, but not all the time. The only person who always carried her pocket watch with her was Mama Hu. That way,

Helen and Sabine could know where their mother was at all times.

"Not Sabine's. We're talking about Edgar's own missing pocket watch," Mama Hu corrected him. "Edgar bought us all pocket watches, but he himself had a special one. It's been missing for thirteen years. Old Man Leung suspected that the pocket watch might be with Gene in his mansion in Hiawassee."

As long as Ming had known Mama Hu, he knew that she could lie at the drop of a hat. Today, she didn't even try to lie to him about where Sabine had gone. Mama Hu stated it all, as though she wanted Ming to go after Sabine.

And that's what I'll do.

"Are you watching the kids?" Ming asked.

"The babysitter's with me, but yes, the kids are going to stay here until Sabine returns."

"Okay. Good. I don't want the kids to wear you out."

"No, no. They're not. Do you want to see them? We're getting ready for lunch. I can ask the cook to make you a Cuban sandwich."

"That will be nice, Mama Hu. I'll be there in half an hour." It would take twenty minutes to get to Mama Hu's house in downtown Savannah, but Ming wanted to shower and change first.

It would give him a chance to talk to Mama Hu in person and elicit more information about what his wife was up to.

After Ming hung up, he replayed the conversation with Mama Hu. Something was off. Sabine wouldn't leave the kids with anyone—not even her mom—without specifying when she'd return.

199

Ming texted Helen to ask her if she knew where Sabine was. Helen didn't reply right away, and that made Ming antsy.

When she finally called him back, Ming was aghast. "My wife did what?"

Before Helen could even explain the entire story, Ming had made up his mind.

He had one day to get to Hiawassee to join the kitchen crew of Skye's the Limit, catering dinner at The Mechanic's mansion.

Their five-minute conversation was all it'd taken for Ming to cancel lunch with Mama Hu and his kids and jump in his truck to make the six-hour-plus drive from Tybee Island to Hiawassee, Georgia.

During the drive, he called Mama Hu and made her spit out everything she knew about the situation. Ming tried not to blame Mama Hu for getting Sabine into the mess.

Edgar Hu had already been dead and buried for years. His death certificate said that the cause of death was "blunt trauma and thermal injuries with smoke inhalation." The forensic pathologists at the Georgia Bureau of Investigations had found carbon monoxide in his blood and soot in his airways. His lungs had charred in the fire and his organs basically cooked, but there were still some tissues internal enough for the coroner to examine.

It meant that Edgar was still breathing when his car was set on fire, in spite of the fact that he'd been near death from the blunt trauma to his head.

There had been no suspect. The single person of interest was Bobby Kane, one of Gene Gilroy's transient garage workers—whose minimum-wage job was to sweep the floor and clean up the tools. However, he had an alibi for that evening, a woman he'd picked up at a local bar. And he died two days later in a motor-cycle accident on a rainy night.

Through the passage of time, the case grew cold due to a lack of evidence. It was the strangest thing. No witnesses, no clues, nothing.

A car on fire on a deserted road, and no one saw or heard it. An early morning thunderstorm put out the fire before a lone motorist finally drove by it the next day and called 911.

Some of Edgar's personal effects had never been recovered. Not his pocket watch, not his satellite phone, and not his wedding ring. They seemed to be things randomly taken to show a semblance of a robbery, but Ming didn't have enough proof of his passing suspicion.

Edgar's murderer might still be on the loose, though nothing could bring Edgar back.

He was dead.

End of story.

It was Ming's unpopular opinion that Mama Hu should've let the past go.

If she wanted to do something about it, she could have asked Ming. His company could use the business. He would have done the investigation and not let Sabine get involved—or at least only be involved behind the scenes.

Not out there facing danger.

He floored the gas pedal.

Once Bitten, Twice Shy (Guardian Sweethearts
Book 1)
JanThompson.com/shy

Guardian Sweethearts
JanThompson.com/guardian

Sign up for book news from Jan Thompson:
JanThompson.com/newsletter

ACKNOWLEDGMENTS

Many thanks to my Georgia Press publishing team for keeping up with my writing schedule.

Thank you to editor Kim Kemery for editing and proofreading this novel.

Thank you to these first responders for answering my questions about real life scenarios. All literary licenses and mistakes are mine.

• Police detective and author Dony Jay, about police procedures.

• Emergency medicine physician and author Dr. John Galt Robinson, about medical emergencies.

A special thank you to my loyal readers who have been with me from the beginning. You've waited patiently for me to write my books, and you never let up over the years. May God bless you!

I am grateful to God for my family's encouragement for my writing career.

And I'll always remember my beloved mother and my late father for having instilled in my brothers and me the love of reading and writing from a very early age. I miss my father here on earth, but I will see him again in heaven some bright day.

Most of all, I am eternally thankful to my Lord and Savior, Jesus Christ, who died on the cross to save me from my sins and rose again from the grave to give me eternal life. Without Him, I can write nothing (John 15:5).

Jan Thompson
John 3:16

BOOKS BY JAN THOMPSON

CHRISTIAN BEACH AND ISLAND ROMANCE

Seaside Chapel (7 Books)
JanThompson.com/seaside
Journeys of Love through Life's Ups & Downs

CHRISTIAN COASTAL ROMANCE IN THE SOUTH

Savannah Sweethearts (12 Books)
JanThompson.com/savannah

CHRISTIAN TRAVEL ROMANCE

Vacation Sweethearts (8 Books)
JanThompson.com/vacation

CHRISTIAN CHRISTMAS ROMANCE IN THE CITY

Midtown Christmas (4 Books)
JanThompson.com/christmas

CHRISTIAN CHRISTMAS ROMANCE ON THE COAST

Christmas Sweethearts (3 Books)
JanThompson.com/christmastown

INTERNATIONAL CHRISTIAN ROMANTIC SUSPENSE

Protector Sweethearts (6 Books)
JanThompson.com/protector
Treasures Lost and Found

Defender Sweethearts (6 Books)
JanThompson.com/defender
Defending the Defenseless Worldwide

NEAR-FUTURE TECHNOTHRILLERS WITH CHRISTIAN ROMANCE

Binary Hackers (4 Books)
JanThompson.com/binary
Cyberthrillers

CHRISTIAN SUSPENSE IN BETWEEN SERIES

Guardian Sweethearts (2 Books)
JanThompson.com/guardian

Subscribe to Jan Thompson's mailing list:
JanThompson.com/newsletter

PROTECTOR SWEETHEARTS

Private investigator Helen Hu and her associates specialize in searching for missing persons and hunting for lost treasures. Join them in their adventure suspense around the world in *USA Today* bestselling author Jan Thompson's Protector Sweethearts, a series of Christian Romantic Suspense with a side of mystery.

Protector Sweethearts is a spin-off of Savannah Sweethearts and Vacation Sweethearts.

JanThompson.com/protector

- Book 0 (Prequel): *Once Bitten, Twice Shy*
- Book 1: *Once a Thief*
- Book 2: *Once a Hero*
- Book 3: *Once a Spy*
- Book 4: *Twice a Fighter*
- Book 5: *Twice a Convict*
- Book 6: *Twice a Soldier*

DEFENDER SWEETHEARTS

Defender Sweethearts is a sister series to the Protector Sweethearts Christian romantic suspense collection. While the heroes in Protector Sweethearts search for lost treasures and lost people, the Defender Sweethearts novels focus on protecting the helpless and hopeless. The main characters in Defender Sweethearts come from the supporting cast in Protector Sweethearts.

JanThompson.com/defender

- Book 1: *Never a Traitor*
- Book 2: *Never a Hostage*
- Book 3: *Never a Fugitive*
- Book 4: *Always a Maverick*
- Book 5: *Always a Champion*
- Book 6: *Always a Guardian*

GUARDIAN SWEETHEARTS

Guardian Sweethearts is a collection of Christian suspense novels in between other books in Jan Thompson's story world. These sandwiched stories feature married couples who met in the books before the present ones. Therefore, the books in this series are both prequels and sequels or preludes and postludes.

JanThompson.com/guardian

- Book 1: Once Bitten, Twice Shy: A Christian suspense novel in between Tell You Soon (Savannah Sweethearts Book 3) and Once a Thief (Protector Sweethearts Book 1)
- Book 2: Check Once, Check Twice: A Christian suspense novel in between Love You Always (Savannah Sweethearts

Book 7) and Never a Traitor (Defender Sweethearts Book 1)

- Book 3: Going Once, Going Twice: A Christian suspense novel that comes after Reach for Me (Vacation Sweethearts Book 2)
- Book 4: Fool Me Once, Fool Me Twice: A Christian suspense novel that comes after Wait for Me (Vacation Sweethearts Book 3)

BINARY HACKERS

Like more suspense with your Christian romance? Like to read suspense thrillers? If you're looking for clean near-future romantic suspense without compromising the Christian faith, these books are for you.

From *USA Today* bestselling author Jan Thompson come these inspirational near-future cyberthrillers combining technothriller and romance, starting with Binary Hackers that feature computer specialists living at the edge of cyberspace, where they have to juggle being law-abiding truth-telling Christians while carrying out their assignments by any and all means possible.

The Binary Hackers series is set in the same story world as Jan's other books, and characters from the other series may make cameo appearances in this series and vice versa.

∾

JanThompson.com/binary

BINARY HACKERS

- Book 1: *Zero Sum*
- Book 2: *Zero Day*
- Book 3: *Zero Out*
- Book 4: *Zero Trust*

SEASIDE CHAPEL

Welcome to *USA Today* bestselling author Jan Thompson's Seaside Chapel Christian beach romance series. These novels are set on real-life St. Simon's Island, Georgia—a beach town where history is all around and the future is a moment away—and the neighboring fictitious Seaside Island, where the rich and famous live.

Savor the small-town atmosphere and the warm southern beaches of St. Simon's Island and the idyllic Golden Isles along the Atlantic Ocean. Enjoy the music of the orchestra and hymns of the church, and hang out with our Christian friends who attend Seaside Chapel, a little church by the sea known for its beach weddings and fair share of love and life.

As these Christians grow in their knowledge and understanding of God, they are tested in their spiritual maturity, their love lives, and their relationships with others. Share their heartaches and healing, and cheer them on as they celebrate faith, family, and friends.

JanThompson.com/seaside

- Book 0 (Prequel): *His Surprise Proposal*
- Book 1: *His Longing Heart*
- Book 2: *His Wake-Up Call*
- Book 3: *His Morning Kiss*
- Book 4: *His Quiet Serenade*
- Book 5: *His Waiting Love*
- Book 6: *His Beach Retreat*

SAVANNAH SWEETHEARTS

Welcome to the new south! From *USA Today* bestselling author Jan Thompson come these clean and wholesome, sweet and inspirational Christian romances set on the romantic beaches of Tybee Island and in the coastal town of Savannah, Georgia. Meet a group of multiracial and multiethnic churchgoing Christians who love the Lord, work hard in their careers, and seek God's will for their love lives. Against a backdrop of ocean, sand, and sun, these inspirational romances showcase aspects of the human need for God and for one another. Have some tea, settle in a comfortable reading chair, and enjoy these sweet celebrations of faith, hope, and love in Jesus Christ.

JanThompson.com/savannah

- Book 1: *Ask You Later* (Artist Romance)
- Book 2: *Know You More* (Multiracial Romance)

- Book 3: *Tell You Soon* (Asian-American Romance with Suspense)
- Book 4: *Draw You Near* (International Romance)
- Book 5: *Cherish You So* (Wheelchair Billionaire Romance)
- Book 6: *Walk You There* (Old-Meets-New Tour Guide Romance)
- Book 7: *Love You Always* (Romance with Suspense)
- Book 8: *Kiss You Now* (Multiracial Romance)
- Book 9: *Find You Again* (Multiracial Romance)
- Book 10: *Wish You Joy* (Christmas-Themed Romance)
- Book 11: *Call You Home* (Deaf Chef Romance)
- Book 12: *Let You Go* (Asian-American Romance with Suspense)

VACATION SWEETHEARTS

Travel with our friends from Savannah, Georgia, to the coast and to the mountains. Cheer them on as they celebrate the immeasurable grace and undeserved mercy of God through Jesus Christ.

The Vacation Sweethearts novels are a spin-off of Jan's Savannah Sweethearts series, and fans will recognize familiar faces from Riverside Chapel, a church in the coastal city of Savannah, Georgia. In fact, we might even visit the beach town of Tybee Island from time to time to visit old friends and beloved families...

JanThompson.com/vacation

- Book 0 (Prequel): *Time for Me*
- Book 1: *Smile for Me* (Beach Romance in the Bahamas)
- Book 2: *Reach for Me* (Romance with Suspense in the Smoky Mountains)

- Book 3: *Wait for Me* (Romance with Suspense on a Cruise Ship)
- Book 4: *Look for Me* (Romance with Suspense in a Florida Beach Town)
- Book 5: *Pray for Me* (International Romance in the City of Atlanta)
- Book 6: *Care for Me* (Small Mountain Town Romance)
- Book 7: *Cheer for Me* (International Romance)

∿

Read *Time for Me* (Prequel) for free:
JanThompson.com/time-free

CHRISTMAS
SWEETHEARTS

Welcome to Christmastown, that holiday decorating company that is now run by Cyrus Theroux and his lovely wife, Amy Untermeyer-Theroux. Their story is first told in *Wish You Joy* (Savannah Sweethearts Book 10), the prequel to this Christmas Sweethearts series.

When this holiday romance series begins, Amy's Christmas Tree Farm and Christmastown have merged their daily operations at their Savannah headquarters.

JanThompson.com/christmastown

- Book 1: *Wish You Faith*
- Book 2: *Wish You Hope*
- Book 3: *Wish You Peace*

MIDTOWN CHRISTMAS

Big city romance, small town feel. Four Christian couples minister at Midtown Chapel in metro Atlanta, and Midtown Village, the community of tiny homes for needy families. From November to January every year, this place turns into a Christmas Village for a small-town feel right there in the metropolis of Atlanta, Georgia.

JanThompson.com/christmas

- Book 1: *Let Me Hold You* (Levi Theroux and Maggie Jacobs from *Pray for Me*)
- Book 2: *Let Me Adore You* (Erika Song from *Look for Me* and Hiroki Yamada from *Walk You There*)
- Book 3: *Let Me Honor You* (Forsythia McDevitt from *Call You Home* and Owen Grayson from *Find You Again*)

- Book 4: *Let Me Love You* (Leila Patel from *Find You Again*)